BIG BODIES OF ALL SIZES

Gay Muscle Erotica

PETER SCHUTES
CHUCK IDGAF

Four delicious tales that will inspire you to snatch, clean, and jerk!

World's Biggest introduces Bob "Fork" Follett, a weightlifter with a small problem. When he moves away to join the Varsity Powerlifting team, he discovers that his massive arms, tree-trunk legs, and perfect behind are like Spanish Fly to men. He doesn't need to be big to win the heart of Jed, a divorcé with a gigantic problem.

Steroid Steve is a fictionalized "true" story. At Gold's Gym in Venice, CA, during the 1970s, bodybuilding was getting big. Straight bodybuilder "Steroid Steve" has a little problem. He catches the eye of Peter Schutes, who has quite the opposite issue, as many of us know. When Peter turns on the charm, they find a perfect fit.

Coached tells the story of Luke, a college wrestler with a fondness for hairy bears. His coach, his roommate, and several other influential men help see him through a sexual awakening that sparks and ignites his passion for men of all shapes and sizes.

Enjambment is one of Peter's last short stories. Using a unique form of hypnotic suggestion, he seduces straight Darrell, a gym-goer with a curiosity about Peter's sizeable bulge. Completely under Peter's spell, the young heterosexual returns to his apartment, where Peter discovers he's not the only one with a massive size problem. Keep reading for the twist at the end!

CONTENTS

❧ I ❧
WORLD'S BIGGEST

by Peter Schutes

PROLOGUE

To the average man, penis size may not seem like a big deal. It is an all-encompassing obsession for those at extremes of tiny or huge. Many men with extremely small penises believe they cannot perform the expected duties. When they discover something between their butt cheeks that attracts men, like flies to honey, they get the added bonus of appreciation. The biggest men tend to be drawn to the smallest. Our protagonist Bob was deeply ashamed of his size until he discovered French Active and Passive Greek. Suddenly, both his holes were sources of extreme pleasure.

SIMILARLY, MEN LIKE JED WITH TOO MUCH BETWEEN their legs are ashamed when women reject them. The ladies all say they want a big one, but they turn tail and run when it's a monster. His wife left him with blue balls every night. When Jed discovered Bob's natural talents for stretching and accommodating, he indeed found paradise.

. . .

MOST MEN CLAIM THEY WOULD LOVE TO POSSESS A massive cock. If they knew how lonely they would become, they might remain happy to be somewhere in the middle. Bob was unique: he understood and overcame his shame of being so tiny. His weightlifting skills made him a natural for taking the very biggest. He knew how to switch off pain and supplant it with pleasure. He was proud to be tiny down there. Jed, too, outgrew his shame and humiliation once he found the perfect fit.

FORK

Bob Follett had a neurotic obsession with size. He was one of the unlucky who was cursed with a two-inch erect penis. Growing up, he was constantly comparing himself to other boys. With horror, he watched as his school friends hit puberty and got that sudden growth spurt, making their little Vienna sausages into ballpark franks. Bob was a big boy with a big frame. He took out his frustrations in the junior high school gym, where he marveled as his muscles grew. He was the butt of many jokes in the showers. He didn't let that stop him from lifting weights after school when he could shower in peace without prying eyes and cruel jeers.

In high school, he was singled out for a spot on the powerlifting team. As a freshman, he towered over his team members. The constant weightlifting had a positive effect on his self-esteem. As he grew stronger and bigger, he thought less about what was between his legs. His teammates were intimidated by his towering frame and god-like strength. He didn't shower with his teammates. He didn't want his little secret to get out among them. He would give anything to have another inch, but it wasn't possible. So he grew what he could.

Bob graduated with a full scholarship to the State

University. He rented a room in the college town that summer and got a job in a warehouse. He was tall and strong enough to reach the highest shelves and pull down heavy boxes like they were empty. One of his coworkers, Zeke, nicknamed him 'The Forklift' or 'Fork' for short. The name stuck. Fork Follett was a college kid, but he fit in with the townsfolk like one of their own, even if he was a bit of a snob. His coworkers invited him to countless parties, swimming holes, and topless bars. He refused them all. His obsession with his little dick kept him from getting close to people.

Another obsession was forming in him at the same time. He wanted to see big penises—massive ones. As the summer wore on, his mind wandered into deeper fantasies. He wanted to shove those big cocks down his throat. He wanted them in his ass. He didn't know where this was coming from. It disturbed him. His family talked about such men. They called them 'perverts' and 'faggots'. They were all going to hell to burn in a lake of fire.

GETTING WOOD

One Saturday, Bob went to the hardware store. While he was looking for woodscrews, a short young man approached him.

"Hey there, Fork, you need some help?"

Bob blushed. "Uh yeah, I'm building a bookshelf. You got any wood screws?"

"I'm Roger." The bold youngster stuck out his hand. "Come this way."

Roger walked him through the types of bookshelf construction and wood.

"Oh, I already got the wood," Bob said.

He caught Roger looking below the belt. "None that I can see." The shop clerk gave a friendly laugh, but Fork's mind swirled with fear and shame. How did he know? What did he know?

Roger put a hand on Bob's massive arm. "I see a brick shithouse but no wood."

Not realizing the implications, Bob asked, "Do you carry any wood?"

Then he got the surprise of his life. Roger pinched a section of his pant leg, revealing the outline of an enormous, throbbing cock. "Only the wood you just gave me."

Things moved very fast. Roger unlocked the storeroom door. They entered. He locked it. They were all alone.

"What are you into?" Roger asked.

"Excuse me?"

"Doesn't matter. I got the biggest dick in the county, and I want to fuck your face, then make you take it up your ass. Sound good, Fork?"

The powerlifter nodded. He was terrified. He never wanted anything so much, and yet he wanted to see his family in heaven someday. He gave in and went to his knees. He had to sit on his heels to get low enough to align with Roger's waist. He watched eagerly as the short man exposed inch after inch of his hard cock. Bob cursed God for making him this way, but his blasphemies were overwhelmed by the lustful clanging in his ears. He put Roger's bulbous head in his mouth. It was easily four times bigger than his own.

"Yeah, just like that." Roger held Bob's head as he pushed in deeper. When he got to the tonsils, Bob gagged.

"Easy, there. It's okay. Mind over matter."

Bob could relate to that. Mind over matter was how he lifted two hundred pounds. Could he control his reflexes?

He spat up a bit of his breakfast to answer his own question.

Roger was a good coach. "Just let it sit there a while longer. Breathe."

Bob did as he was told, and his gag reflex settled down. It didn't vanish completely, but he had mastered it for the most part.

Then Roger pushed past the tonsils, letting inch after inch of his enormous cock slide down Bob's throat. Bob couldn't breathe. Roger rubbed his cheek and shushed him.

"I won't let you suffocate, Fork. Just tap my leg when you need air."

Bob tapped Roger's leg immediately. The log of flesh retreated, and Bob took in great gulps of air.

"Come over here." Roger led him to a soft bench.

"Lie on your back and let your head hang over the edge."

The hulking athlete lay flat on the bench, head dangling. Roger stepped forward, holding his impossibly large tool with both hands. Slowly, he forced his way past Bob's tonsils until his balls met his nose.

"This may feel bad initially, but you'll like it." Without any warning, Roger brutally fucked Bob's throat. Bob was uncomfortable, but it was nowhere near as bad as deadlifts. Roger stopped suddenly and groaned, unleashing a flood of semen into Bob's throat. Bob had no choice but to swallow it. He fought to expel it, only to have it come out his nose.

Roger was still rock hard. He walked around to the other end. He got something off the shelf and spread it all over his cock.

"What's that?"

"Baby oil." Roger's cock was shiny and slick. "Take off your pants."

Bob was so afraid Roger would see his little nipple of a dick, but he did it in phases, so his shameful crotch was still hidden in his underwear.

Roger spat into his hand and wiped it on Bob's puckered hole. He put baby oil on the opening and used a finger to work it in. It felt nice.

"This is easier if I just go in all at once. Is that okay?"

Bob nodded. Roger lined up the head of his cock with Bob's butthole, then immediately shoved the entire length of his cock into the bodybuilder's hole. Bob saw stars and made a sound like a goat being slaughtered.

"Does it still hurt?"

Bob nodded vigorously.

"How about now?"

Bob nodded again. He realized he was mastering the pain. Some of those endorphins he produced during deadlifts were back at work, turning his ass from a throbbing bundle of raw nerves into a stretched, aching butt.

"How about now?"

Bob shrugged. Roger was not one to stand on ceremony. He immediately began to piston in and out of the giant. Bob was surprised at how good it felt to be invaded like that. He was such a masculine man in many respects, but his tiny penis meant he would have to give pleasure to men like Roger. And that gave Bob pleasure in return.

Without warning, Roger pushed up Bob's underwear with the intent to jack him off. What he saw shocked him.

"Oh my god, it's so tiny!"

Bob struggled to free himself from Roger's cock and his gaze of wonder.

"No, no, Fork. Stay put. Some guys like serving forks, but I like oyster forks. You dig?"

Bob nodded. By now, the back-and-forth motion of Roger's cock was downright pleasurable. All the pain of his initial entry had subsided. He was left with a growing warmth inside. It started to tickle, or maybe he had to pee. He wasn't sure how to describe this completely new sensation.

"You like it, huh." Roger winked.

"I feel so good."

"So do I," Bob said. "It's like a hundred times better than pussy."

"I wouldn't know." Bob looked away.

"Fork, it's good we met. I heard about you from the guys at the warehouse. I had a feeling you would check off all the boxes."

"What boxes, Roger?"

He smiled. "Big and strong, check. Willing to take my huge cock, check. A tiny penis, check."

"They told you I have a tiny penis?" Bob wanted to cry.

"No, that was a happy surprise."

The tingling in Bob's belly was growing more intense as Roger pounded harder and deeper. At one point, Roger pushed past some inner wall with a loud pop. He kept doing it over and over.

"You were so big; I didn't know if I would reach."

Bob would have asked more, but the continual violation of that valve at the end of his rectum created a pleasure so intense it prevented him from forming coherent words. Roger put the giant's legs on his shoulders. They were heavy but didn't stop Roger from violating the deep hole inside Fork.

Fork shuddered. Something was happening. He had never masturbated, so he didn't know what was happening. He also had never had a dick inside him, so he didn't know what else was happening. His innards began to quiver until they broke out in spasms of pleasure. The contractions were not lost on Roger.

"Oh fuck, you're one of those. Check another box."

Between convulsions, Bob asked, "Another what?"

"You got girl parts in your guts. A lot of the teenie weenie guys are like that. You're having an anal orgasm, and it feels so fucking good on my cock."

Bob jerked involuntarily, letting the waves wash over him.

"Oh shit, I'm close." Roger slowed his pace. But Bob kept spasming, and it would push Roger over the edge.

When the first hot spray was released inside the bodybuilder, it intensified his spasming and caused a rush of burning sensation to flood his tiny penis. The second spurt was three times as much as the first. Bob's bowels were coated with slick, gloopy cum.

As Roger's ejaculation continued beyond all reason, something new happened to Bob.

His tiny penis reared up, then shot a quarter cup of cum all over Roger's shirt. Roger collapsed onto Bob's massive frame. He licked the big bodybuilder's nipples, which caused Bob to cum again.

"Oh, Fork, you're perfect."

"I don't really know what just happened."

Roger laughed. "You had an anal orgasm and then shot your load."

"You weren't horrified by my tiny penis?"

"Au contraire, mon frere. It turns me on. I'm so big, and it gets me hot when a guy is small. If he's tiny, it's like a dream come true. I don't like guys with big dicks. But I can tell you do. I have a little clubhouse where big guys like us get together. You should come by sometime."

THE CLUBHOUSE

Bob limped home to work on his bookcase. His life was forever changed. He realized there was a place for him in the wide world of sex. He liked big dicks, and always wanted one of his own. But now he had learned that having a big dick inside was far superior. And his little dick could shoot a lot of cum. And probably best of all, he could have an orgasm in his bowels. He wanted to try a million more giant dicks.

He took off his clothes at home and looked at himself in the mirror. He was big and strong. His face was handsome. Below the belt, he was shamefully small. He turned to the side and marveled at his beautiful ass. He had never realized how big and desirable it was. If getting fucked meant going to hell, he was happy to burn.

The next time Bob got together with Roger was at the clubhouse. Every eye was on him when he walked into the dimly lit shed.

"Uh, is this?"

"Priapus Club. Welcome." An extremely handsome older man with a thick cock outlined in his tight jeans extended his hand. "Jedediah. Jed is fine."

"Bob, pleased to meet you."

"Oh, we all know who you are, Fork. Our club has been waiting for someone like you."

"Like me?"

"Yeah, big, powerful, with a little dick and the ability to orgasm internally. We're a very focused club."

Bob smiled. "I guess you found me. Which ones are the small dicks?" He looked around the room.

"You're the guest of honor."

Bob looked at the six crotches around him. They were all bulging obscenely. He grinned. "I already took the biggest dick in the county, so this will be easy."

Everyone laughed. "Is that what that little shrimp told you?" Jed wiped tears out of the corners of his eyes. "He's not even seven inches."

"He's the biggest I've ever seen," Bob said.

A slightly cross-eyed guy with a beer can hat leaned forward. "You ain't seen nothin' yet. Wanna beer?"

Bob shrugged. "Sure."

The cross-eyed guy named Mike brought over a cold one. After he put the can in his left hand, he pulled Bob's right hand down to his leg. "Feel that? Thicker'n a beer can."

Bob gasped. He could compare. His fingers nearly touched, holding the beer can. He couldn't get halfway around what Mike was packing.

"Holy shit, Mike."

Mike smiled. "I ain't the biggest. Maybe the thickest."

Bob was introduced to all the members. It was a standard greeting for Bob to grope the guy and size him up.

"So, how do I fit in the club?"

Jed said, "You're our bottom bitch. We're gonna fuck you inside out."

Roger came in. "Bob! I was hoping you'd come."

Bob leaned into Bob's ear. "I think they all want to fuck me."

Roger smiled. "Do you want that to happen?"

Bob blushed, then nodded.

"We're going to fuck you so good; you'll never know what hit you. To help with that, take this."

Roger held up a yellow pill that read 'Lemmon 714'.

Bob hesitated. "I don't do drugs."

Roger said, "Trust me, you'll want a Quaalude. It will open your pussy right up."

Bob didn't like the pussy remark. 'It's my ass."

"Sure, Bob. Sorry. But listen, once this gets started, you're gonna see, hear, and feel a lot of things you might not like without this." He twirled the pill and caught it, opening his hand. Bob smiled and took it with a swig of beer.

As Bob's eyes adjusted to the dim lighting, he saw a few things he wasn't sure about. One was a pillory. Another was an oversized hanging leather hammock. He squinted and saw a few whips hanging from a rack.

"I ain't into pain like that."

Roger smiled. "There are other clubs that meet here. All you need to concern yourself with is the sling. He pointed to the hammock. "Why don't you go over there and try it out, Fork?"

Bob shrugged. He walked over to the sling and sat in it. Jed came over and helped him lie back so his head hung over one end and he could put his feet up in stirrups on the other.

Bob noticed the wedding ring on Jed's finger.

"Yeah. I'm married. She don't put out."

Bob frowned. "I'm sorry, brother."

Jed patted his rump. "Okay, get those clothes off. Don't worry; we all crave little dicks like yours. You got nothing to be ashamed of."

$\maltese$ 4 $\maltese$

ZEKE

The door opened, flooding the clubhouse with light. Zeke, another coworker from the warehouse, came in. "Am I too late to fuck Fork?" Zeke was the guy who gave him the nickname.

"No, Zeke, you're right on time. We're watching the colossus get naked."

Bob got a little dizzy when he bent down to untie his boots. He stumbled to remove his clothes as the dizziness gave way to mellow disorientation. By the time he shucked off his underpants, he was glowing. The whole room applauded, which only made him feel better. He climbed back into the sling, putting his thick, muscled legs in the stirrups. As he looked around the rooms, he saw the men massaging their crotches or, in some cases, their legs. He felt a deep sense of brotherly love for these men. He rubbed his own pectoral muscles, amazed at how big they had grown since junior high. Jed stepped forward with a tub of Albolene. He generously applied it to Fork's massive asshole and stretched him with a forefinger.

"Shoot, he's tight." He handed Bob a handful of tiny glass vials wrapped in netting. "If you feel pain, pop one of these and inhale. It will help."

Bob was giddy now. He put his hand on Jed's lips. "I like you, man."

"You're gonna like me a lot more by the end of the night. He grabbed the log of flesh on his left thigh as emphasis."

"Show me now." Bob pouted.

"We got an order. It makes it a lot better for you, trust me."

The order started with Zeke, who was very big, big enough to scare off most comers but not gigantic like Roger. Zeke stepped up to the sling, rubbing Albolene on his cock. "Fork, I've wanted to fuck you since the day you walked into the warehouse to apply for a job."

"Wishes really do come true." Bob was pretty loopy now.

Zeke pressed against Bob's puckered hole. It didn't give way, so Zeke spanked Bob. That caused the hole to pucker and then gape a little. Zeke pushed in partway.

"Go the whole way!" Bob was a demanding bottom.

Roger nodded. "He's a weightlifter. It's better for him, gets the endorphins going."

Zeke pushed in all the way until his pubic hair rubbed against Bob's fleshy buttocks.

Bob grunted. He was aware he felt pain, but it was like he was hovering over his body, watching himself feel the pain. The endorphins flooded his brain, mixing with the Quaalude. He pinched his own nipples and moaned. Zeke knew a willing bottom when he saw one. He fucked without mercy, banging over and over against the rear wall of the rectum. The pressure from Zeke's thick meat squeezed his bladder repeatedly until he pissed himself. There were cheers. Apparently, Zeke's ability to fuck the piss out of a man was legendary. Bob was too high to be embarrassed. In fact, he was proud. He was proud of himself but especially proud of Zeke for his unique talent.

Although Bob wanted to tell Zeke this, his mouth

wasn't cooperating. He made animal sounds instead. Zeke picked up the pace. Bob wanted to feel Zeke pop past that hole deep inside, but he realized Zeke didn't have what it took. He was good, but he was no Roger.

Zeke's sweat trickled into Bob's mouth. Bob writhed in mock orgasm. He wanted Zeke to feel as good as Zeke was making him feel.

Seeing Bob in the throes of anal orgasm surprised Zeke so much that it put him over the edge. "Oh shit, I'm gonna...I'm gonna." A flood of cum filled Bob's rectum. As a kind of thank you, Bob shot one of his legendary buckets of cum all over Zeke. Zeke collapsed, withdrawing his cock. He kissed Bob on the mouth. Bob had never kissed, but he felt like an expert.

❧ 5 ❧

GANG BANG

Roger was next. He said, "I like fucking a cummy ass."

Bob held up a finger and said, "Check!" They both laughed. The Quaaludes dissolved any awkwardness from their first encounter. Roger forced his way balls-deep into the giant man. Bob was loosened and familiar with Roger's anatomy. He played with Roger's nipples, which caused him to pick up the pace. At last, his cock reached its maximum length, and he popped past the hole.

Bob bucked and wheezed. "Fuck, ungggh! Coming inside, man." He couldn't form complete sentences and wasn't even sure he had properly formed his words.

But Roger nodded. "Anal orgasm, brother. You're welcome."

The spasms in Bob's guts brought Roger to orgasm almost immediately. Hot ropes of cum filled his rectum, mixing with the cooler sperm from Zeke.

To his surprise, Bob shot a load on Roger without touching himself even once. Roger didn't want to kiss. When he pulled out quickly, it caused cramps deep inside Bob. The muscular giant writhed and twisted as Roger walked away.

Before the orgasms could subside, another club

member came forward. He was shy and wore a wedding ring. He had auburn hair and sea-green eyes. Freckles kissed his cheeks. He was by far the best-looking guy in the room.

"Hey Fork, I'm Sean."

"Hey, Sean. Welcome to my asshole." They both laughed. Sean shucked off his clothes, revealing freckles on his shoulders, chest, and soft cock. Even flaccid, it was a monster. Sean kneeled and put his lips on Bob's asshole. He sucked and struggled until Bob farted out the cum. When Sean stood up, he was rock hard. It was thick, long, and looked painful. Before Bob could protest, Sean pressed his way into the giant ass. He kept pushing until he popped past the inner hole. Then he pushed some more. Bob had never felt anything this deep. His anal orgasm began immediately, massaging the freckled cock inside him. Sean held on to Bob's waist. He thrust in and out with tremendous force. He liked to pull out completely and then go back in to the hilt, staying there a minute to let the orgasmic contractions stimulate his massive cock.

Sean was beyond the hole and in some new place that quivered even more violently.

"Shit, Bob, you're gonna get me off like that." Sean stayed in place until the vibrations were too much to bear. He pulled all the way out with a smacking sound, then went all the way back in with a loud pop and shot his semen somewhere well beyond the rectum. The nerves up there were so intensely wired that the hot cum made Bob cry out.

Sean looked into Bob's eyes. "Are you okay?"

Bob pulled him to his lips to kiss, but Sean pulled back. "I don't go for that stuff."

Bob, giddy on ludes, said, "Well then, come around so I can blow you. It's better than a kiss."

Sean shrugged and walked to the other side, choking Bob with his half-inflated freckled cock.

While Sean broke past Bob's tonsils, Mike came forward. The angle of Bob's head prevented him from seeing more than a glimpse of the man as he took off his beer-can hat. Bob saw Mike remove his shirt, revealing rippling muscles on a lean frame. Bob was curious to see what Mike was packing when he shucked off his jeans. But with his mouth full, he couldn't ask Mike to show him the prize. The thickness of Sean's cock was comparable to Roger's. Bob was so relaxed; Sean could fuck his throat with abandon.

Mike took one of the glass vials out of Bob's hand. "You're gonna need this." Bob did his best to nod with Sean's salami down his throat. There was a pop and tinkle as the glass broke. Mike held it under Bob's nose. The room went dark. Bob was high above the clouds, but he came crashing down when Mike forced his cockhead into Bob's rectum. It felt twice as thick as any cock yet. Like someone was pushing a wine bottle up inside him. Bob grabbed the vial and sniffed hard again. He relaxed and was vaguely aware of Mike finding his way to the end of Bob's rectum. That was as far as he could go. He was either too short or too thick to pop his way past that magic hole. Bob reached down and felt the exposed length of Mike's flesh. He had a good two or three more inches he could go. Bob was good and loose now, so he twisted his hips and pulled Mike inside him all the way. The valve felt stretched to its breaking point, but it allowed the massive cockhead to enter. Mike's eyes lit up with astonishment.

Bob smiled to himself. He was pleasuring two huge cocks at once. He looked up at Sean, who looked away. "No eye contact."

Bob tweaked Sean's nipples. That was apparently okay because Sean gasped and bent at the waist. Bob went to work on Sean until, at last, he came. It tasted like powdered sugar frosting. Sean pulled out and walked away. Bob was about to swallow the sweet cum when Mike grabbed and kissed him, letting some cum into his mouth. They kissed until they had swallowed all of the cum.

Mike said, "I've never...never had anyone, girl or guy, take me all the way."

"Is that why you kissed me?"

Mike grinned. "Nah, I just heard that Sean's cum tastes like frosting, and I wanted to find out myself." They both laughed.

"Is this okay?" Mike was humping Bob slowly, pushing in and out of the inner hole.

"You can go faster if you want."

Mike grinned. "I wanted this to last forever because it's never gonna happen again."

"Why? Are you going to kill me at the end of all this?"

Mike snorted. "No, but we've never managed to keep a member all the way to the end of the night and no repeat customers. It has to do with Jed and Boomer."

Bob hadn't met Boomer yet. But he knew Jed was packing something massive down there.

Mike said, "Okay, I'm gonna fuck you full speed." When he turned up the tempo, Bob basically went blind. He was in such deep ecstasy; he just saw white. He felt his rectal muscles shiver with orgasm over and over as Mike grunted and fucked him harder and harder. When Bob regained his eyesight, Mike's hips were moving in a blur, faster than any fuck yet.

Mike became aware of the intense massage he was getting from Bob's guts.

"Is that..."?

Bob nodded. "Anal orgasm."

Bob heard other members of the club gasping. They all knew that they had to push past the rectum to set one off. Another member of the club, Leonard, came over. "Dude, are you going in all the way?"

Mike was very close to orgasm. He gritted his teeth as he nodded. Bob had never been filled so completely. Just for kicks, he took another whiff of the popper and then put it under Mike's nose. Mike blasted deep inside Bob before collapsing on top of him. He grinned and held Bob's head so he could kiss him for real.

"You changed my life, man."

Bob shrugged. "All in a day's work."

❧ 6 ❧

LEONARD

Leonard was next. He had a tooth missing, but otherwise, he was pretty cute. He had shoulder-length blond hair and big ears that poked through. Bob continued his survey of his newest suitor. He wore baggy trousers that disguised whatever he might be hiding. He dropped those trousers, revealing a soft cock that hung beyond halfway to his knee. It was bigger soft than some of these guys were hard.

Leonard had a charming laugh. "Don't worry; it don't grow none. It's a show-er."

Sure enough, the cock stood up hard but barely changed size. It did get thick enough that Bob felt the need for poppers again. Leonard placed his slender cockhead at the cummy entryway. Leonard had a small head, but his main shaft was beercan-thick. As he slid his way in, Bob's hole gradually stretched wider. When the first sharp pain signal alerted Bob to the invasion, he broke open the poppers and inhaled deeply. The room disappeared, and when it returned, Leonard was banging on the rectum wall. The very thickest part of Leonard's cock was the middle, and it was stuck, painfully stretching open Bob's hole.

Bob scooted to one side, suddenly allowing Leonard to gain entrance to that promised land beyond the rectum. Leonard gasped in surprise. A single tear trickled down his cheek when his balls slapped against Bob's butt. He was in all the way, which was a huge relief for Bob.

Plowing with abandon, Leonard's cock was the first to find another miracle - the descending colon. The second his cock bumped into it, Bob went into full anal orgasm, more intense than any he had experienced yet.

Leonard looked worried because Bob was gasping and seizing, but Bob reassured him he was fine. "Never been better." This was carte blanche to fuck even harder and faster, making Bob moan louder and louder.

"Leonard, oh fuck, what is that? Why is it so good?"

Leonard didn't answer. The truth was his dick did get bigger if he was really excited. Bob realized this when both the frequency with which he felt intense pleasure at the descending colon and the intensity with which he felt pain increased dramatically. He had to crack open a new vial of poppers because he had inhaled the other one completely.

Leonard leaned close, "I should warn you; I take a long time." Bob reached up and pinched Leonard's nipples.

Leonard shook his head. "Not wired that way."

Bob asked, "Are you going to get any bigger?"

Leonard nodded.

Thirty minutes passed, and Bob was almost tired of the intense orgasm that wouldn't stop. Bob had an idea. He soaked his finger in spit and wriggled it into Leonard's asshole.

"Oh shit, oh god, is that what it feels like?"

Bob held back a laugh. A finger and a kielbasa are very different. He kept his cool. "Yeah, Leonard, pretty much."

Leonard's eyes rolled back in his head. "That feels so fucking good!" Bob's muscular fingers were long and thick. He put a second one in, and Leonard nearly collapsed. When Bob got a third one in, Leonard came. He dribbled at first, but each successive pulse of his penis brought a bigger and bigger payload. By the time Leonard had finished, he had spattered the descending colon with semen. His cock shrunk back to its previous size and softened. The peristaltic action in Bob's colon made Bob 'shit a dick.' Leonard's boa constrictor snaked and slithered out the hole, followed by a long parade of semen. Bob cupped his hand and drank some of it. He could taste Sean's sweet frosting mixed in with all the others.

Leonard kissed Bob on the head and said, "Good luck."

JED

When he saw Jed disrobe, Bob understood why Leonard had wished him good luck. Jed had gray hair and salt and pepper pubes with a truly enormous cock. It was in a different league from all the other men before him. The monster hung down to his knee, and soft, it was bigger around than a soup can. It was almost as big around as a coffee can. Bob trembled from a mixture of arousal and fear. He loved big cocks, which was beyond any typical definition of big.

"Do you want to throw in the towel?"

Bob shook his head vigorously. "I made it this far; I haven't reached my limit yet."

"Do you need a break?"

Bob smiled. "I already took a piss. I'll be fine."

Jed appeared more afraid than Bob. An idea leaped into Bob's head out of nowhere. "Jed, why are you hesitating? I'm willing."

Jed smiled sadly. "The last person who said that didn't survive."

Bob wrapped his hand partway around Jed's soft cock. "I can handle it. Look at me. I'm a fucking giant. My insides are big enough for you."

Jed surveyed the muscular frame. "I suppose you are bigger than most guys, body-wise anyway."

Bob felt a sting. He was so much smaller where it counts. As he cradled the base of Bob's impossibly large cock, he marveled at God's cruelty. One man was so small, the other so enormous, and neither of them could get the job done. Bob stroked Jed's monster until it grew even larger.

Bob hefted the cock into position. "I'm ready." He popped another vial and inhaled the contents deeply. Jed was hard. He smeared Albolene on the hole to further lubricate it. There was so much cum in Bob that it helped Jed gain entry. As a steady trickle of cum dribbled out of Bob, Jed used it as a lubricant to push his way in. Bob took a second whiff. The pain was excruciating.

"Am I hurting you?"

Bob shook his head. It was a lie. Fiery lightning bolts shot through him. He sniffed and sniffed until he lost all connection with his body. When sensation returned, he was in agony. He thought about the 225-pound deadlift. He thought about the 300-pound deadlift. He had made it to 300 at least three times. Jed was just 275. He could do this.

Bob pulled Jed close so that his cock snaked its way in further. He leaned and steered Jed's cock past the rectum and down to the end of the sigmoid colon. As Jed throbbed and more blood hardened his gargantuan cock, he grew longer and thicker. His head touched the bottom of the descending colon. Then he turned the second corner.

Bob saw fireworks. His whole body trembled as his inside muscles stroked and massaged Jed's meat.

"Oh, oh shit. Oh, holy shit." Bob realized Jed was a virgin, and this was his first orgasm. He could feel his insides swelling with the hot liquid. Jed kissed Bob deeply. He didn't give a shit about his wife in that moment. He just wanted to be one with Bob as the last droplets of cum escaped his massive slit. He stayed inside Bob, kissing him passionately.

Bob felt that pride you get when you beat your personal best. It eclipsed the intense pain of having his asshole stretched like a gym sock. Even soft, Jed was too thick. Bob figured that with enough practice, he could take him easily. That's how weightlifting works. You reach a plateau, but you surpass it. He knew someday he could painlessly take Jed inside him and feel only pleasure. He made up his mind to do just that.

Mike still had Boomer to deal with. How could he be bigger than Jed?

The answer came; he wasn't. Not really. These men had never taken a cock up their ass. They just measured the length and decided, based on one-dimensional criteria, that he was "bigger." They didn't consider girth. Boomer had a lovely long cock that hung well below his knees. But it wasn't quite beercan-thick. It looked impressive but couldn't hold a candle to Jed's girth.

Boomer was ruggedly handsome. He had spiky black hair and burning blue eyes. He had been watching the action with Jed and couldn't believe his good fortune. In the club's history, they had never made it past Jed, the showstopper. Boomer looked like a man who had been refused all his life. He was about thirty, and though not a virgin, he never found a woman that could handle him more than once. Bob could tell all this just by looking at him.

Boomer grinned. "You ready, son?"

"Yes, Daddy." It was so absurd; they both laughed.

Boomer was still soft. As he got hard, his girth increased very little, but his length nearly reached the floor. Boomer enlisted Bob's help to guide his cock into the loose, sloppy hole. It went in like a letter being passed through a mail slot. Quickly, the serpentine cock wriggled its way through Bob's lower digestive tract. When it hit the magic button at the descending colon, Bob's insides, still recovering from Jed, fired to life. The spasms stroked Boomer's cock like so many feather boas being dragged along its length.

Boomer grinned. "Shit, kid, that feels good."

"It's mutual, believe me." Bob's eyes fluttered as Boomer started to climb the descending colon. The orgasms intensified. He was just thick enough to stretch the walls, sending Bob into sheer bliss.

Boomer said, "I'm almost in. I'm in! I'm all the way in!" He kissed Bob on the forehead.

Bob smiled, "Good, now fuck me."

What happened next was so purely pleasurable that Bob lost consciousness. Boomer had a powerful downstroke. He could only pull about halfway out without walking backward, so he contented himself with a rough pounding. The last portion of his entry, the colon, was tender from all the friction with Jed. Bob was orgasming in a faint. When he came to, he shot a load of cum on Boomer's chest and belly and coated the top of his cock. Bob could feel some of his own hot cum slide inside, riding the train that was Boomer's cock. It was sublime. Boomer looked proud. He had never gone all the way, and he'd never made a man or woman cum. It was probably the best day of his life.

While Boomer humped in and out, Jed came around and laid his cock across Bob's lips. Bob felt something flutter inside that had nothing to do with Boomer. It was the way Jed looked at him, grateful, wanting something more. Bob opened his mouth and took the pink prize into his mouth. It was only half the head. Nobody could take more. Or could they? Bob remembered that after his injury when a weight had cracked his maxilla, he discovered he could lock and unlock his jaw like a snake. He hadn't ever thought to try it for sex. He wiggled his jaw, and it fell open, letting the whole head past his lips.

Jed looked astonished at what came next. Bob inhaled him inch by inch, forcing the cock head down his throat. Bob had never been prouder. He was giving Jed a present he'd never dreamed possible. When Jed was at the bottom of his throat, Bob massaged the remaining length with both hands. When he gagged and spit came out his nose, he used it as lube. He tapped Jed on the leg, signaling he needed air.

Jed wasn't familiar with the signals. He was so absorbed in the pleasure that he failed to notice Bob turning blue. Boomer finally spoke up.

"Hey, Jed! Give the kid some air!"

Jed woke from his reverie in horror. He pulled out, but Bob wouldn't let him pull all the way out. He took three deep breaths, never ceasing his massage of the exposed length, then pulled Jed's cock down his throat again. Jed fucked his face, but he paid attention to the hand signals.

Boomer was turned on by the blow job taking place across from him. He fucked harder and harder, fascinated by how it affected the speed with which Bob stroked Jed's monster. He got just that little bit harder, enough to hit a new spot deeper than before. Bob's spasms reached a fever pitch. Boomer tried to slow down to keep from coming, but it was too late. Stock still, buried to the root in the boy, he shot the biggest load of his life, and it was the first time he came inside of somebody. Tears rolled down his cheek. He wanted to kiss the boy, but his mouth was full. Bob pushed out Boomer's cock involuntarily. It was followed by a loud fart and a river of cum.

Seeing the growing pool of cum on the ground beneath Bob was the catalyst for Jed's orgasm. It built in his loins, then spread to his balls and down the length of his shaft. Jed shot down Bob's throat. Bob tapped for air, and this time Bob let the head pop out. He held it close to his tongue, but it sprayed his face and hair with hot cum. The ejaculation lasted forty-five seconds and left Bob coated in cum.

A round of applause brought Bob back to the present moment. All seven men surrounded him, each cursed with a dick that frightened away women and men. Bob was fearless. He wanted all of them inside him. He wanted Zeke, with his thick cock, so thick it fucked the piss right out of him. He wanted Roger, who had taken his cherry, showing him how he had sexual value after all. He wanted Sean, no-kiss Sean, with his beautiful, freckled cock. He wanted Mike, the slightly cross-eyed man who learned today that he could go all the way, no matter how big and thick he was. He wanted Leonard's everlasting cock that reached the magic spot when it got hard enough. He wanted Boomer, with his long serpentine cock, longer than anyone else but not too thick. He wanted Jed more than any of them. Jed was married, but Bob longed to be held in his arms, rocked to sleep at night, fucked silly every morning.

What Bob didn't know was that Jed wanted Bob to himself. He didn't give a fuck what his wife said. She could watch for all he cared.

The applause died down. Bob grinned. "So, how often do you guys meet?"

JED OFFERED BOB A RIDE HOME. BOB THOUGHT HIS heart would break. He sat silent as Jed navigated the clean streets of the college town.

Jed spoke up. "I'm getting an annulment."

Bob was shocked. "What? Why?"

"We never consummated the marriage, obviously."

"Not even the tip?"

Jed laughed and shook his head. "She's agreeable. She wants to spend her life with a man, not a circus freak."

"I... uh...I want to live with a circus freak." Bob blushed like a schoolgirl.

Jed smiled. "I think that can be arranged."

MOVING DAY

Jed's powerful muscles were covered in sweat. He was lean, with a thick beard, and Bob loved watching him walk. The baggy jeans couldn't hide the long, fat cock as it strained against his pant legs. It was moving day. Jed and Bob made a great moving team. They were both strong, one freakishly so. Whenever Bob bent to pick up a heavy box, his ass made Jed hot. Bob couldn't help but notice Jed's unbridled lust and the swelling it caused. The hungry stare made Bob's hole hungry. He had hosted Jed in his asshole dozens of nights throughout the summer, even before the annulment was final. Each time, it got a little easier. He didn't need Quaaludes anymore. He rarely needed poppers, but they always kept some on hand just in case. They went through two large tubs of Albolene that summer. Bob's hole was really loose. Sometimes when Jed licked it to warm him up, a little red apple popped out. Jed would push it back in, but not before he put it in his mouth and licked it. He felt guilty, so he never told Bob about it. It was Jed's fault. He fucked Bob every night for weeks until one night, that thing popped out.

Bob was the happiest he had ever been in his life. Jed fucked him six ways to Sunday. Every time Bob felt him pop past his sphincter, it was a point of pride. Nobody else could satisfy Jed like he could. Now they were going to live together. Jed's ex-wife moved back home with her folks, leaving plenty of room for a willing sex slave to live there.

Jed had been preparing a surprise for Bob. He fixed up the basement with a sling. If it were up to Jed, Bob would live in that sling. But the boy was about to start college, so he wouldn't see that dream fulfilled until Winter Break. He was going to lock that boy in the sling with handcuffs then.

Bob didn't want his own room. He wanted to sleep with Jed.

"If you do, your ass is never gonna close up."

Bob said, "That's what I was hoping."

The boy got his wish. And true to his word, Jed didn't miss a night of fucking. Sometimes he fucked Bob twice or even three times. The boy needed his sleep, so he made sure they started early.

Jed took Bob to Cracker Barrel on the last day of summer vacation for breakfast. He liked watching the big boy wolf down thousands of calories. It turned him on to think about the food converting into muscle and fat. He loved this young man with the perfect body to accommodate Jed's gargantuan cock.

After breakfast, He took Bob shopping for notebooks, pens, paper, and tight gym shorts. At home, Bob tried on the stretchy green nylon shorts with white piping. His ass swallowed the seams. His massive thighs strained against the hems. His crotch all but vanished in the mountains of muscle all around. His belly was a washboard. His huge pecs looked ready for suckling. Jed wanted him right then.

"Turn around for me."

Bob obediently spun around.

"Pick up that pen you dropped."

Bob bent down, exposing hard, muscular buttock

flesh through the shorts. Jed could even see the dimples on the sides. He was getting trapped in his jeans. It was just a matter of practicality if he needed to take them off. His log of flesh sprang upwards, grazing Bob's hard ass.

Bob stood up; his butt cheeks ate the shorts, revealing the path to paradise. Jed stepped forward until his hard cock brushed against Bob's thighs.

Bob stood stock still. He let Jed do all the work.

Jed extracted the fabric from between Bob's buttocks and yanked them down quickly. Jed needed two hands to pull down his own pants to get past the enormous dick. Bob's petite penis showed no resistance. It didn't even reach as far forward as his thighs.

Jed wanted him completely. Bob relaxed and moaned while Jed suckled on his tiny prick. Jed had eaten a lot of pussy, but it couldn't hold a candle to Bob's little man-clit, with the aromatic balls exuding hormones that made Jed overflow with lust,

He turned his attention to the gates of paradise. Parting the muscled flesh, he jammed his tongue into the loose slot. Soon his nose was in there too.

Bob groaned, "Jed, I want you to fuck me. Bad!"

Jed snatched the Albolene from the kitchen counter and bent Bob over the table. The bow was so massive that he nearly covered the entire kitchen table with his bulk.

Jed wanted to see his lover's expression when the massive cock e termed him. He flipped Bob onto his back, legs raised high.

"Put it in me, daddy."

Jed pushed past the loose opening and wound his way through Bob's bowels. He watched as Bob's eyes rolled back in his head. A huge grin spread across the strongman's face. His chest heaved with anticipation. Jed clamped his mouth over a nipple and sucked it. Bob began to orgasm inside.

Jed had been gentle at first, but by the end of the summer, he was free to ravage Bob completely. He fucked hard, forcing his way into the colon and out. Bob moaned like a gale-force wind. He was in such an intense state of ecstasy; it was all his mind and body could manage. The throbbing vibrations in his bowels were building to a crescendo. To Jed, it felt like fucking a giant angry sea anemone.

Bob ceased his moaning, replacing it with a long "Ooooh" that went up and down in pitch depending on the direction of Jed's thrusts. He grabbed desperately at Jed's back until he brought him to his lips. They stayed locked in a resonant circuit peppered with the slurping and sucking noises of sloppy ass and giant cock.

Bob shot a load on Jed's face and chest. Jed licked it up.

"Mm. Like frosting."

Bob smiled with his eyes fluttering. He was steeped in bliss, unable to use words,

Bob sucked in his belly. Jed marveled at the outline of his cock pounding far up inside Bob. If he put his hand in the right place, he could rub himself through the layers of muscle and flesh. This proved too much.

Jed threw his head back and shouted, "Fuuuuuuck!"

He felt something wet. Bob was coming a second time, completely hands-free. Jed paused, allowing Bob's contractions to finish him off. Jed released a steaming hot load of cum somewhere near the descending colon. It followed him as he pulled out. Capfuls of Jed's sperm ran like a waterfall out of Bob's destroyed ass onto the kitchen floor.

They locked eyes and kissed.

"I love you, Bob."

"Me too!"

❧ 10 ❧

GARY

Bob's first day in college was overwhelming. He had to go through three orientations before getting his schedule. The schedule was straightforward: Math, English, Biology, Philosophy, and Powerlifting Team in the late afternoon. Every minute he was away from Jed was torture. He was addicted to Jed and his enormous cock. He thought about it all day in class. His grades suffered a little, but he wasn't worried. His coach was the only instructor who told him to pay better attention.

Most days, practice would end at 6:00 pm, but occasionally, it would go an extra hour. The coach refused to stick to a schedule. Jed came every day to pick up his lover. Bob thought Jed was bored waiting in the bleachers, but the truth was that Jed got off looking at all the powerlifters in their shorts and singlets. The only thing Jed disliked about the late practice was how it cut into his sex time with Bob. By October, Bob had found the sling. He was only too willing to climb in and let Jed have his way with him. If it got late, Jed would fuck Bob piggyback upstairs to the bedroom. Jed weighed 185 pounds, but Bob could carry him like a light backpack. And Jed was so hung, there was plenty of room for error. He never slipped out.

In November, the lifting coach took a job offer out in California. With the State Finals coming up, this would have been a devastating blow, but it was an unexpected bonus. The new coach, Gary Merrill, was a former champion. He was past his lifting age, in his early forties. But Father Time had been kind to him. He was bulging with muscles, and he had something rare bulging as well. Bob could smell big cock from nine meters. Gary Merrill was well-hung.

Bob loved Jed. They had an understanding. At the clubhouse, Bob was for everyone. Everywhere else, he was Jed's property. He could see why Jed wanted that arrangement. Jed could hardly go out and fuck somebody else. Nobody but Bob would be able to take him.

Bob was thinking about this arrangement when he got to the locker room. Since his sexual awakening, Bob was proud of being small. He took showers after practice with all the guys. Most of them were small, too. A few had a decent average cock. But the coach was the only lifter Bob had ever met who was hung like a horse. At least, he thought so; he had yet to verify his imaginings.

Practice ended early, and Bob had nowhere to be until Jed arrived. He grabbed his towel and went to the communal showers. He proudly stepped under the hot water stream and looked around at the other athletes. Average, average, nice but not huge, small, small, average. Then Gary Merrill walked in, his towel slung over his shoulder. He was completely naked. Sure enough, his cock was huge. It rivaled Jed's. The coach couldn't keep his eyes off Bob, who stared back with his jaw hanging. The coach switched spigots to stand next to Bob. The freshman was measuring Gary in his mind.

"Take a picture; it will last longer." Gary grinned, eying Bob's puny penis.

"I could say the same, couldn't I?"

Gary nodded. "I need to see you in my office after

this." Bob glanced at the clock. It was 5:15 pm. He didn't have much time.

"Is this about what I'm thinking it's about?"

"You got it, kid." He dried off and wrapped the towel around his waist, hiding the appendage. Bob was still wet when he got into his clothes and ran upstairs to Gary's office. He knocked on the door.

"Come in, Bob."

Bob gasped when he walked in. Gary's monstrous penis was hard as fuck and standing up against his belly.

The coach spoke. "I know you could never handle this, but maybe you could just suck me off a little?" The coach had the weary sound of a man like Jed, who got rejected for his big penis at every turn.

Bob grinned. "You got lube?"

Gary smiled cautiously and opened his desk drawer, taking out a tube of KY Jelly. "Lock the door."

Bob lay face up on the desk, and Gary ate his ass. He fondled Bob's tiny penis and moaned. Then he stopped. "You're gaping wide open."

"Yeah, uh, the guy I live with, he's as big as you."

Gary slicked up his cock and forced it in. Bob was spoiled on Albolene. KY Jelly was cold and inconsistent. Still, Gary found his way to the sigmoid colon before they reached a dry spot. Bob put more KY on the exposed shaft, and it slipped in easily, moving past the sigmoid colon. By now, he was so used to the involuntary orgasm that he just moaned. But Gary's eyes were saucers.

"How are you doing that?"

"Don't know. You went deep enough to push the button."

Gary stood still and let the peristaltic waves massage his colossal prick. He moaned softly. After a time, he gently swung his hips back and forth, pressing the orgasm button repeatedly. I realized he was getting thicker at the base. It really started to hurt. He thickened until Bob thought he would burst. Gary was a strongman with a cock that rivaled Jed's. And he was balls-deep inside Bob. The young man was so excited that he shot a load that splattered the papers on Gary's desk.

"Hands-free? Did I do that?"

Bob nodded.

"You're my first, Bob. First in my whole life!"

Bob pitied the man who had never found his Bob like Jed had. "That sucks."

Gary laughed. "No, it's fucking wonderful. I'm gonna use you every chance I get."

Bob wondered how Jed would feel about it.

"Oh, Jesus Christ, I'm coming! I'm coming inside you!"

The coach exhaled as a torrent of warm cum filled Bob's guts.

COMING CLEAN

Bob debated telling Jed about the encounter with Gary and the possibility of more. Jed didn't seem willing to share except at the club. The club wasn't taking any new members, so it was the same menagerie of characters each time.

On the truck ride home that night, Bob could feel Gary's cum trickling out, staining his pants. He took it as a sign to come clean.

"Jed?"

"Yes, Bob?"

"You know the new coach, Gary Merrill?"

Jed nodded.

"Yeah, well, I found out he's got the same problem." Bob was afraid to say more.

"Same problem as you? Poor fucker."

Bob shook his head. "Same problem as you, Jed."

The silence was deafening. Bob felt compelled to fill the empty air.

"I saw him in the shower after practice."

Jed looked angry, but his voice was calm and kind. "I don't own you, Bob. I would like to, but I don't. If you want to fuck the coach, I won't stop you."

Bob frowned. "Yeah, but will it hurt you?"

Jed smiled. "I share you with six other guys every month. I can share some more. You're like a public treasure. Your ass is a thing of wonder."

Bob felt relieved. But he hadn't come completely clean.

"Jed, I'm sorry, but it happened so fast. He fucked me."

The older man took a deep breath. "You got any left for me?"

Bob nodded.

"Good. If it feels like a spanking, just go with it."

That night Jed put Bob in the sling and fucked him using only Gary's drying cum as lube. It hurt, but Bob felt he deserved it. Jed was a professional fucker now. He did tricks that made Bob piss himself. He dug so deep that Bob shrieked. Jed slowed down after that. Whatever anger he felt had subsided.

Jed decided to lube up. He pulled out fast and was shocked when a stream of blood poured onto the floor. Luckily, it was just a capillary. The bleeding stopped.

"I feel like a monster." Jed hung his head.

Bob rubbed his tummy and stroked his cock. "You're my monster. You're a good monster."

Jed chuckled. "Can I fuck your throat since the back door is out of business tonight?"

In reply, Bob leaned back, opened his mouth, and unhinged his jaw.

It had been a while. Bob gagged a couple of times, but he stuck with it. Jed found a rhythm that had a curious effect. It was a throat orgasm. Bob felt the thick meat stretching his throat in such an even rhythm, and suddenly he was tingling there. The throat contracted and expanded to match the rhythm of Jed's thrusts.

"Bob, you're a fucking miracle."

Bob did his best to nod in agreement.

Jed let the contractions finish the job. He gave Bob five seconds to catch his breath, then forced his way back down the boy's throat. He held his cock there for a while, letting the contractions bring him over the edge. He pulled out and splattered Bob with cum. Bob lapped up as much as he could. The rest covered his face like frosting.

❧ 12 ❧

THE SCHEDULE

Bob let Gary fuck him on Tuesdays and Thursdays. He was inexperienced like Jed had been, so Bob acted as his teacher. He taught him how to make him piss, the moves that would turn on the vibrations of orgasm. When he gave Gary a blow job, it became his favorite. He fucked Bob's mouth so much that the boy grew hoarse. Bob didn't mind.

The affair came to an end temporarily for Winter Break. Gary went home to Ohio for Christmas. Bob talked to his family and convinced them to let him stay with Jed over the break. As agreed, Bob climbed into the sling and let Jed handcuff him. He could only get out for bathroom breaks. Jed had a few surprises he hoped would excite Bob. First, he brought in a warm enema and emptied it into Bob's bowels. Bob cramped and writhed but wouldn't go until Jed allowed it. After ten minutes of torture, Jed relented. Bob emptied his bowels completely. He'd never felt so clean. It didn't take long for Jed to soil his insides with cum. This led to another bowel cleanse. Bob loved it, but he pretended to be suffering. Bob rushed to the toilet. Jed came in. Don't flush. He checked the bowl. It was crystal clear, save for a large quantity of cum.

Jed filled Bob a third time, but he didn't unlock Bob this time when he gave up.

"Just let it go."

Jed kneeled to lick Bob's butthole. Suddenly, a clear torrent of water came gushing out.

"Oh, Jed, I'm so sorry!"

Jed smiled. "For what?"

Another kink he wanted to explore was stuffing. He bought a croquet set. He lubed up his boy's ass and shoved the balls in one by one. He watched, pulling on his meat, while Bob pushed out eight croquet balls.

"I wish I had a movie camera. We'd be millionaires."

Every day Jed thought up something new. The croquet balls were too easy, so he shoved a half dozen softballs inside Bob. They were less slick than the croquet balls, so Bob really had to push to get them out. After the sixth one, the red rosebud peeked out and then retreated.

Bob never tired of the attention Jed lavished on him. He felt worshipped. He hoped Jed felt worshipped too when he took him deep inside his throat or his guts.

The days in the sling blurred into each other. Jed used Bob for pleasure, and Bob felt pleasure in the giving. It was different from many things in nature. A lion eats a zebra. The zebra gets no benefit whatsoever. But Jed takes all the pleasure he wants from Bob, and Bob has more pleasure than when they started.

❧ 13 ❧

LOGJAM

In Spring, Gary announced they would attend the New York City powerlifting conference. Bob was excited. He felt guilty leaving Jed alone with no one to fuck. Jed had begun to subscribe to some strange magazines. One of them, Straight to Hell, was their favorite. They both enjoyed the articles and advertisements.

As Bob was packing for the bus ride to New York, Jed was fingering through Straight to Hell. He jumped out of his chair.

"Look at this, Bob!"

He pointed to an advertisement: "World's Biggest Dick Pageant Grand Prize $1,000.00".

The date coincided with the Powerlifting conference. It was obvious Jed had to go. There couldn't be anybody bigger than him. Longer, perhaps, but not bigger. Bob confirmed that there were several categories. One for girth, one for length, and one all-around biggest dick. That was Jed's contest, for sure.

Jed booked a room in the YMCA where Bob was staying. They only had single rooms, so they couldn't room together. He dropped Bob off at the bus and caught a train.

The Powerlifting conference was exciting for Bob.

He saw so many masculine guys lifting. Gary Merrill came from this world. He was legendary. Not just for his many wins but also for his monster cock. Some of the older folks saw him, stamped their feet, and neighed. Gary loved it. He'd always been proud of his huge cock. Now that he had met Bob, he even had a use for it.

Bob realized it would be awkward if Gary and Jed met. At 4 pm, Bob and the team went back to their rooms. A few minutes later, Bob heard a knock.

He said, "Jed, is that you?" and opened the door. It was Gary.

Gary pushed his way in. "Bob, I need to fuck you now. Is that okay?"

Bob hesitated. He didn't know what would happen if Jed showed up. He shrugged. "Yeah, come in."

Bob shucked off his clothes and lubed up his asshole. Gary was getting very good at fucking. He knew the patterns and rhythm that maximized Bob's pleasure. He had learned to grind and twist to hit all the right spots. If anyone asked Bob who was better, Jed or Gary, he would have said, "Both."

Gary found the low bed the perfect height for fucking downwards, his favorite. He made Bob squirm and sigh with joy.

Suddenly came a familiar knock. "Bob, you in there?"

Bob had forgotten to lock the door. It swung open, revealing an astonished Jed.

Gary asked, "Who's this?"

Jed said, "Shut up. Get under him." He wasn't hostile. He was excited. He whipped out his dick which gave Gary a thrill. With Gary lodged firmly inside from below, Jed pushed his way in from the top. It was a real logjam. Bob was certainly not tight, but this was like trying to put a bowling ball in his ass.

Jed snorted and pushed down hard. Bob's ass made a

sharp pop, like the first time Roger fucked him. Jed was in. Bob bit down hard on his knuckle to keep from crying. But then something happened. As Jed's cock slid along Gary's, Bob's rectum expanded, bringing a unique pleasure. The pressure made him piss himself. Gary was a bit unhappy about getting a soaking, but it was much less important than feeling his dick twin rubbing against him. This was a first for all three men.

Bob choked a sob when Jed passed through the colorectal valve. That little hole was stretched far beyond its capacity. But it was very elastic, and Bob adjusted to the new, fuller feeling. His orgasms, which stopped the minute Jed knocked, were starting back up. Wave after wave of anal orgasm made him quiver. Gary was fucking from below, pushing the button and making everything more intense for Bob.

Jed was all the way in beside Gary. Bob rocked back and forth, stroking the two cocks with his stretched insides.

Jed pounded with a newfound intensity. Gary matched his strokes, but on the way in while he was on the way out. The friction of the two horse-hung men rubbing cocks was too much. When Bob shot the biggest load of his life all over the room, the two men sighed and released their semen. Bob was flooded with two loads of cum. Gary said, "Holy shit!" As the two men grew soft, Bob's guts desperately pushed them out. The two cocks popped out one after the other, followed by an obscene amount of cum.

Bob wiped his brow and felt his tender rectum. He wasn't going to walk right for weeks. But it was the best fuck of his life.

"Gary Merrill." The coach extended his hand.

"Jed."

Gary smiled. "I know a little about you. Your reputation is similar to mine." he gestured towards his monstrous soft cock that rivaled Jed's. But Jed was a grower and a show-er. So you couldn't judge the flaccid cocks.

Jed said, "Yep. I'm huge. I heard you were too. You are."

Gary squinted, "Jed, what's your relationship to Bob?"

Bob blurted, "We're boyfriends."

Jed corrected him. "We're a common law marriage, but it's an open one."

Bob had never heard this. Jed was pissing on his territory.

Gary borrowed some dry clothes from Bob. They were both hulks, so it was a good fit.

Jed said, "Bob, that contest is tonight. Are you going?"

Gary interrupted. "Straight to Hell Night? Oh god, I love it. I'm entered in the WBD."

Jed spelled it out. "World's Biggest Dick. Hmm. May the best man win." He couldn't be resentful towards a coach who was transforming Bob into a Powerlifter and whose cock he had rubbed with his own. Neither man was sure who was the biggest. Not even Bob could be sure. It was going to be a photo finish.

❧ 14 ❧

WORLD'S BIGGEST DICK

S traight to Hell Night was decadent, artsy, and lewd. Cocktail waiters walked around in nothing but a bow tie, their wieners wagging. The drinking age was 19, so Gary bought a round of beers. Bob and Jed didn't drink much, so the beer went to their heads. Out of the corner of his eye, Bob recognized someone from home. It was Boomer. He came over, talking excitedly.

"I'm gonna win longest; I know it."

Jed said, "Why not biggest?"

Boomer put a hand on Jed's shoulder. "My friend, you are the biggest at the club. I'm the longest. It's different."

Gary couldn't make out the outline of Boomer's meat. Because Gary had been unable to fuck, he had spent his sex life as a bottom. The bigger, the better. He wanted Jed badly, but Boomer sounded intriguing.

"Young man, your clothes are hiding the prize."

Boomer smiled and grabbed his cock, pressing it against his baggy pants so an outline appeared. It was missing a few inches but it was enough to make Gary's butthole pucker with anticipation.

Nightclubs in New York are very, very late starters —the bars close at 4:00 AM, so events sometimes don't get started until long past midnight. Jed stopped drinking, but Gary, Boomer, and Bob were three beers in when the master of ceremonies took the stage to preside over the penis pageant.

"Ladies. I mean, Lady and Gentlemen." There was laughter. The only woman in the place was a bartender. "It's my honor to preside over the most exciting pageant on Earth. Yes, that's right, the inauguration." A few more laughs.

"No, but seriously, this is the world's only contest of its kind. Get ready because we will be unleashing a colossal show for you. It's going to be enormous! Will the contestants come backstage now for a pre-judging? I'm kidding. The element of surprise is everything. But we need you, seriously, so come on back!"

Jed, Boomer, and Gary left to get ready. Bob was all alone. A handsome college grad sat down beside him. "Not entering?"

Bob shook his head and held up a pinky.

The man laughed. "I would enter, but they don't have a grower category."

"I think there is. I remember reading it on the poster out front."

The man stood up. "Oh, good. I go from less than one inch to seven and a half inches. If they don't judge the final size, I might win. Wish me luck! Oh, how rude; I'm Hoyt." He shook and didn't wait for Bob's name.

The pageant was well-organized. Every contestant was asked the same three questions.

Have you ever been turned down because of your size?

What sets you apart from the average man?

Top or bottom?

Gary had the best answer to the first question. "No. Never. My ass is the perfect size."

Jed's answer to number two was sweet. "I'm lucky

because I found a man who can handle me, and I get to fuck him every night." He waved to Bob, who blushed.

Boomer was more matter-of-fact. "The distance from my cock to the ground"

When Hoyt answered "Versatile" to number three, the crowd shouted, "BOTTOM!"

There were a dozen more contestants, many of them looking like last place just from the bulge in their trousers (or lack thereof). But a few were real whoppers.

The Emcee ordered the contestants to the back room. He looked out at the audience. "Okay, men, this is where we help these titans to reach their maximum potential. Come backstage if you want to help. The floor emptied out. Bob led the pack.

When he got back to the dressing room, it quickly descended into chaos. Grabbing hands and wagging cocks met and shook in salute. It was dark. Bob couldn't see well. His hands bumped into mammoth cocks. Was it Bob? He slid his hand along the length and knew it wasn't anyone he knew.

"Your hands are so soft. I'll bet your mouth is soft." The stranger was an outline in the darkened room. Bob worried that he wasn't helping Jed. The stranger was gentle but firm. He put his hand on the back of Bob's head and brought him to the tip of his throbbing cock. Bob opened his mouth and took the musky cock into his mouth. He used his hands to shove the cock down his throat.

"No gag reflex, eh? You like deep throat?"

Bob nodded as best he could with his throat full of rock-hard dick.

The stranger pivoted his hips, giving Jed many opportunities to breathe between stuffings. Bob's throat began to vibrate involuntarily. The stranger gasped.

"You're gonna make me come, boy. I gotta stop." He yanked his dick out of Bob's throat and kissed him behind the ear before sauntering to the next willing mouth.

Bob continued his search for Jed, who was no doubt desperate for Bob's talented mouth. He heard a familiar grunt. It was Jed. He was fucking somebody. It was Coach Merrill.

"Jed, I want you to come inside me."

Jed replied, "I'll bet you do, Gary. You want me to lose the contest."

Gary was very hard. Bob unhinged his jaw and wrapped his lips around his coach's massive dong. He moved quickly, getting Gary in as far as possible. It set off the vibrations.

Gary held Bob's head and forced himself deeper until he was all the way in. Bob pulled back and took a giant breath before swallowing Gary completely. He moved his head up and down, adding to the pleasure he gave with his undulating throat muscles. The next time Bob came up for air, he tasted that salty clear liquid that meant a man was about to come. He knew he should stop so Gary would keep his hardon for the contest. It was Gary who pushed Bob's head back down. Bob stood still. He tried to help Gary but couldn't stop the muscles from pulsating.

"Oh god, shit, Bob. I'm gonna lose."

After Gary spurted out the last of his cum, he pulled Bob to his lips and kissed him. "Your man will win, but I'll be close behind."

Jed said, "His ass is so loose, it's like fucking a gym sock."

The emcee turned on the lights, and the modest sluts pulled their clothes on. Jed pulled out of Gary. The coach's long, softening cock spit out another glob of cum.

At the sight of his boyfriend's throbbing cock, Bob got a pang of regret that he hadn't sucked him. But judging by his size, Gary had maxed him out. He was huge. Now he just had to keep it.

Bob watched from backstage as Boomer, Gary, and Jed marched proudly. Judges took notes. Jed did a handstand, hitting himself in the face. It made him look huge. Gary stroked himself gently, and his member began to swell and lengthen to a nearly impossible size. Jed's size was incomprehensible. Judges came with tape measures and took measurements. It took a while because they needed to give a few men a chance to get hard again. Boomer was, far and away, the longest cock in the show. Attention excited him, and he had grown to his maximum size. He was fat around but not as fat as Jed by a long shot. Jed's cock hung to his knee, but Boomer was down to his calf. It was too huge to stand up. In the "show-ers" section, Hoyt was clever. He had avoided any sex at all backstage. He had soaked his cock in ice water. It was tiny, almost as small as Bob's. When Hoyt took the stage, the whole audience booed.

The emcee came to Hoyt's defense. "Don't forget; we've got a growers category." Hoyt looked at Jed and licked his lips. He was imagining dirty things, no doubt, because swiftly, his nipple of cock grew into a banana. A big banana. The crowd cheered. Hoyt must have won, but the judges were still doing calculations.

"Ladies and Gentlemen, we have a clear winner in the length category. Would Boomer Evans please step forward?" Boomer was half hard. He swung his cock between his legs to get the blood moving. It grew to its impressive length. Men were throwing their business cards at Boomer. He grinned and stepped back in the line.

"Hoyt is our most impressive grower." Hoyt stepped forward, grinning. His cock was at rest in retreat. He rubbed it a dozen times, and it swelled to its unbelievable size. The crowd roared. Hoyt stepped back in line.

We have an exciting tie in two categories. Jed

Bledsoe and Gary Merrill are in a dead heat for Thickest and Biggest. We need the audience to decide who's biggest. The runner-up will be the thickest."

A drunk patron cried out, "How do we decide?"

The emcee smiled. "You're each invited to hold them in your arms and decide for yourself. If you have an injury, don't try to lift them." There was a table with ballots. In an orderly but lustful fashion, the crowd filed onto the stage, squeezing, shaking, slapping, and weighing. Jed was rock hard. He loved the admirers. Bob knew that apart from his competitor Gary, none of the people in the room could give Jed pleasure with more than their hands. So he wasn't jealous.

The Emcee took the stage for the last time. "The ballots have been cast. World's Thickest Cock is awarded to...Gary Merrill. Jed Bledsoe has the World's Biggest Dick."

Despite his prowess, Jed was a bashful country boy at heart. He smiled and nodded as men handed him business cards. Some scribbled notes on the back of the cards. Bob wondered what they could be.

❦ 15 ❦

THE WINNER'S CIRCLE

Jed pulled on his overalls, ending the incredible display of manhood. He shuffled over to Bob, still hard in his pant leg. "I got a thousand dollars, just like they said."

"What were all those men with cards about?"

"Porn scouts, mostly. A few were rich guys who wanted to pay to play with me. A couple of job offers." Jed patted his chest pocket, which was thick with cards.

Bob said, "Don't they know you're too big?"

"Apparently, there are some experts out there."

Bob felt panic. He would lose the love of his life to porn or some rich guy. He wasn't Jed's only option now. There was Gary with his monster cock. There were the nameless men in California who were wide open deep bottoms. Bob began to cry, much to his chagrin.

"Hey, what's this about?" Jed cradled Bob's head in his hands. "It's no big deal. You're my world, Bob. Nothing can change that."

Bob sniffed. "But you want to fly away and fuck a bunch of strangers on camera for money."

Gary wandered over to eavesdrop. Jed said, "Not one of those guys is gonna mean anything to me. I'll make enough to buy us a nice house with a pool. You're all I care about. I'm doing it for you."

Bob rolled his eyes. "You're going to fall in love with someone else."

Gary stepped forward and interrupted. "Bob, this man loves you. The whole time he was fucking me, he talked about your beautiful tiny penis and how disgusting mine was. All those porn stars are hung, even the bottoms."

Jed raised an eyebrow. "Really? They all got big dicks? Yuck. I'm gonna need Bob on set to keep me hard."

❧ 16 ❧

HOTEL ORGY

The three winners, Gary, Boomer, and Jed, escorted Bob back to the YMCA. The air was thick with sexual longing. Bob's, Jed's, and Gary's rooms were too small for an orgy. Boomer was staying at an actual hotel, so they squeezed into a cab and rode uptown to Boomer's place. Like so many, it was a tourist hotel, but the rooms were much larger than expected. Boomer had a King-sized bed, big enough for all four of them. Bob felt needy, so he hogged Jed to himself, and Boomer fucked Gary.

In Jed's mind, it was a waste of a precious resource - Bob. His boy was able to handle all of them. He wanted to share. Boomer couldn't quite squeeze the last few inches into Gary, who was a lifelong bottom but built differently than Bob. When Bob saw the disappointed look on Boomer's face, he felt guilty. He relented, letting the full orgy break out. With Jed stuffed fully in Bob's ass, Boomer added his cock. Bob had taken Gary and Jed earlier, so this was easier. Boomer was thick: huge by most standards, but nothing like Bob and Jed. Boomer slid along the length of Jed's monster, stretching Bob to satisfaction. Then, when he slid past Jed and filled the descending colon, it brought on a wave of contractions, each one more intoxicating than the prior one,

Bob leaned back and unhooked his jaw, letting Gary slide down to a point halfway between his tonsils and his stomach. The contractions in Bob's throat muscles massaged Gary's thick tool. He moaned softly. Bob tapped for air. Gary pulled out, waited a few seconds, then went all the way back in. Somehow that set off a body orgasm in which all of Bob's involuntary muscles were throbbing, squeezing, stroking the three cocks inside him. Bob was in paradise. Boomer had plumbed the depths and found several magic buttons. Cum shot out of Bob like it was his first time. Boomer grinned. He knew his length had caused Bob to shoot his load. He was one-third right. The ecstasy of being completely and deeply filled at both ends was what had sent him over. Boomer was the deepest, Jed was the biggest, and Gary was the thickest. It was sheer bliss.

Bob came again in bucketloads, coating all three men with his sperm. Boomer was first. He was in the firestorm of contractions, further than anyone else could go. The constant stroking and squeezing on his cock as he slid back and forth, coupled with the incredible sensation of sliding along Jed's dick, was enough to put him over.

"I'm gonna come."

"Okay. Do it. Dump in my hole."

Boomer was so turned on by that last remark that he unloaded twice his usual helping of cum. Bob could feel the hot liquid as it sprayed and sprayed for much longer than expected. He slumped over Bob's chest, wedged so tightly inside him that he had to wait for Jed before exiting.

Gary was next. He was so excited to be with huge-hung men like him, using this boy who was nothing like them, with his tiny penis like a new mushroom sprouting from a log in the forest. Gary envied him. He touched the boy's massive nipples, as big around as a silver dollar. Bob jerked, startled by the intense pleasure Gary's touch brought him. He shot a third load, no smaller than the previous. It seemed like his tiny balls could hold a lot of semen. That was what sent him over: thinking about having a tiny penis that could cum like Bob's. "Oh Bob, good lord, I'm gonna..." He didn't finish his sentence. He gave Bob a high-protein meal directly in his stomach. He pulled out, allowing Bob to breathe. His softening cock hit Bob in the eye. Bob licked the pearls of extra cum off the apple-sized head.

Jed was the last. With Boomer caught between him and the exit, he knew he would have to end the intense pleasure he felt fucking Bob and stroking Boomer with his cock. Jed knew Bob could get off one more time. He played with the little pecker, pinching, fingering, and squeezing him. Bob responded by wriggling and twisting. Still, Jed kept playing with the man-clit, imagining his own was equally tiny and insignificant. When the first clear, sticky drops came out of Bob, Jed licked his fingers like it was candy. It was pungent, almost like a lemonade.

"Bob, you taste so good."

Bob was too excited to respond. His little cock stood at attention, throbbing. When Bob came that fourth time with no hands, it pushed Jed over. The cum flew over Bob's shoulder and landed in Jed's eye. It burned, but it turned him on. He started fucking furiously, causing Boomer to swell and lengthen inside Bob. He emptied his balls into the young weightlifter, filling his sigmoid colon with his seed. Boomer saw the incredible fourth ejaculation and felt his cock get slippery with Jed's cum. Jed was still fucking at an alarming rate, and it was all too much.

"Fuck, man, I'm gonna cum again." Boomer sighed and let loose another load inside Bob. Jed slowed, then stopped. The two men stayed inside him, waiting to soften, but they were too turned on.

Gary said, "Is there room for me?"

Bob said, "I'm stuffed full, and you want to put the world's thickest cock in me?"

Gary nodded.

Bob shrugged. "Come inside."

It was tricky getting a third cock inside of Bob, especially one as impossibly thick as Gary's. Gary was not a top, and he fumbled until Jed's skilled hand forced Gary past the gate.

Bob was in agony. He felt like someone was trying to drive a Mack truck up his ass. But the further in Gary went, the better it felt.

"Fuck me deep, Gary."

Gary did as he was asked. Soon, his cock was wedged up Bob's asshole with the other two. All the commotion of Gary sliding along their shafts aroused both men. Boomer sighed and licked his lips. He was going for a third load. Jed was incredibly aroused. He could see his boyfriend's rectum stretched beyond capacity. He watched as Gary's balls slapped into his. Bob paid the price as the men grew more and more aroused by each other. Gary was wrecking Bob's guts. The rectum and colorectal valve were so stretched that Bob wondered if he would be able to go out without diapers. If he farted, it would never make a sound again. This round was for the three men who had given him so much pleasure. Bob focused on assisting his contractions, which made all three men moan aloud simultaneously. They pulled back a few inches as a unit, then pushed in again, hitting the button deep inside. They matched rhythms, pounding their thick penises into Bob's entrails. Bob helped keep the men in sync so that all three cocks moved in unison, back and forth, in and out. Bob tried to squeeze the cocks at the base by tightening his rectum, but it was impossible. But then contractions in his sphincter started, reaching a fever pitch. Bob thought he was going to shoot his own cum out of his ass; it was such an intense orgasm. The men were in ecstasy. Bob was contracting the whole length of his lower digestive tract. It massaged the knot of cocks and made it throb. The throbbing traveled down the length of each shaft, coaxed by the contractions in the rectum. When it reached their balls, it was time.

"I'm gonna come," Gary said.

"Me too."

"Me too."

The men pawed at each other and Bob, tweaking nipples and kissing with abandon as they came together in the same instant. To Bob, it felt like an enema. To the men who were fucking Bob, it was sheer bliss. Bob didn't need to cum a fifth time in an hour. He was content to provide pleasure for the three handsome men that used him to get off.

Bob waited until the last of the threefold cum had sprayed his guts, then relaxed his sphincter. The soft cocks came squirming out of Bob like three long snakes. Gary and Jed popped out at the same time. Bob's hole snapped shut around Boomer. The worst of the pain was over. He was reluctant to let Boomer go. He tried to trap his head inside him, but he was so loose it was pointless. Boomer's cock hit the floor with a loud thump.

There was an awkward period where the three tops adjusted to the fact that they had all kissed one another.

Gary broke the silence. "I wish we could do this regularly, like monthly."

Boomer, Bob, and Jed exchanged glances. Jed said, "I think that can be arranged."

EPILOGUE

That was how Gary became the only member of the club to fuck and get fucked. Now there were two willing holes, and things went quickly. There was time for combinations—Leonard inside Gary inside Bob. Bob was always the period at the end of the sentence. He was gifted with a small penis, which proved his favorite characteristic. He was a cum slut, and he got all he wanted. There was never any pressure to perform. He welcomed in the massive members of the Priapus Club. He served Jed as a willing hole for him to fill. Jed rewarded him with trips to California. He even got Bob a few gigs on sets where the bottoms didn't have to be hung. Bob was the best fluffer on any set. He could take those huge porn cocks down his throat without batting an eyelid. They made a lot of money in a little time. They managed to steer clear of weed and cocaine and bought a house in Sonoma, where they live to this day. If you go to the town square on Thursday at 2 pm, that's when Jed shops for cheese. If you're lucky, he'll be wearing his tight jeans.

❧ II ❧
STEROID STEVE

by Peter Schutes

PUBLISHER'S NOTE

Gold's Gym in Venice, CA, was the epicenter of the bodybuilding explosion that started in the early 1970s. In this tale, Peter writes about a real person, wholly straight and never interested in him. In fiction, you can turn the tables, as you will see.

STEROID STEVE

I paid 15 dollars for a month's membership at Gold's Gym. I was obsessed with a handsome lifter there, Steroid Steve. I have a fetish for men with small penises, and Steve was truly small. His thick, muscular legs, enhanced by anabolic steroids, caused the tiny member almost to disappear. I got rock-hard every time I thought about him.

I have quite the opposite problem. My cock is exceptionally long and impossibly thick. It makes my back hurt just carrying it around in front of me. Men, particularly those insecure about their size, never hesitate to humiliate me. They call me "gate crasher" or "baloney pony." My least favorite insult is when they brush their feet on the floor and whinny like a horse.

I knew I had no chance of getting together with Steve. He was too small to successfully fuck me, and I was too big to fuck him. He wore a wedding ring and dropped hints about his wife while he was lifting on the main floor.

A few Saturdays ago, I came to the packed gym. I wanted to use the Universal Fitness machine, but every station was three deep with a waiting list. As I approached, a pig-eyed dolt with ugly curly hair made a stomp and whinny. Out of nowhere, Steroid Steve appeared and confronted the ugly freak.

"Hey, Jack, leave the guy alone. He's here to work out like the rest of us."

Jack snarled and walked away. He was big, but Steve was way bigger.

I exhaled. "Thanks, Steve."

He eyed me suspiciously. "I don't know your name. You are..." he extended a hand.

"Peter. Peter Schutes. Your reputation precedes you; that's why I knew your name." As I took his hand and shook, I sounded like a confused schoolgirl.

Steve laughed. "Which reputation is that?"

"I mean, everyone calls you Steroid Steve." I hoped that wasn't insulting.

Steve's eyes drifted below my waistline. "I think I understand why Jack was acting so rude."

I braced for an insult. None came.

Steve said, "I get teased over the same body part but for the opposite reason." I didn't dare tell him that I knew all about it. I just nodded like I was receiving new information.

"What do they say when they tease you?"

Steve sighed. "Cashew, peanut, gnat, you know, the usual. And they are fond of holding up a pinky and putting their thumb on the first segment. That one gets me the most."

"Oh man, I'm sorry." I didn't dare tell him that I found it incredibly sexy. He was straight. Instead, I changed the subject.

"Married?" I pointed to the ring.

He nodded. "Not happily."

My inner seducer couldn't keep quiet. "What makes you happy?"

He patted the front of my pants. "If I could have about a quarter of that, I'd be happy."

Steve's hand on my cock was completely unexpected. I was too giddy to check my words before they came out. "I could probably get halfway."

Steve frowned. "What do you mean?"

Shit. I'd lost focus. "I mean, I'd be happy with half of this. Heck, maybe even a quarter." I grabbed the base of my monster and pinched it, causing it to show through my sweatpants down to my knee.

Steve coughed. "Holy fuck! What do the ladies say?"

"What, ladies?" I let that hang in the air for a while. Steve didn't inquire further.

"Hey, buddy, we're gonna be here all day if we wait for the machine. I'll spot you; you wanna spot me?" He gestured to the huge gym floor with free weights scattered everywhere. Bodybuilders are messy men in general. They ignore the sign admonishing them to put the weights back where they belong.

When Steve bent over to gather the weights we would need, his ass ate his shorts. It was the roundest, most perfectly shaped ass I had ever seen. I stared glassy-eyed at the heavenly butt. I came around when Steve caught me looking.

"Take a picture. It'll last longer. And it'd probably fetch a good price on mail order." I was relieved he didn't call me a fag.

We worked out for a good hour. Steve lifted three times the weight I did. I could barely spot him; the bar was so heavy. He spotted me with one finger. It was a testament to all the Lord gives and all he takes away. At the end of the workout, we hit the showers.

Saturdays meant that stalls came on a first-come, first-served basis. They were all taken. Steve and I both knew better than to go to the open showers where all the regular guys washed themselves. We were freaks in their eyes. They would harass me with envy and Steve out of a sense of superiority. There was no need for either of us to say this out loud. It was a lifelong condition for both of us.

Finally, two stalls opened up at the end of the row, opposite each other. I took the left, and Steve took the right. Some clumsy oaf had torn my shower curtains. Steve's was no better. Because we were at the very end of the row, we didn't have to worry about prying eyes. I lathered up, spending a long time on my cock. Steve spent most of his time on his big, beautiful ass. I wondered if he was sending signals. Then he whistled.

"Damn, motherfucker! Is that soft?"

I nodded. "But if you keep washing your ass like that, it's gonna get bigger." And it did. I went from big to huge, then huge to monstrous. Steve's eyes were riveted on my cock. He licked his lips.

He rubbed his thumb up and down his ass crack, eying my meat hungrily, eyebrows raised. He turned, and I could see his tiny penis was at attention. I wanted to suck it so badly.

Steve said, "I live in Culver City with my wife."

"I live in Santa Monica alone."

"I'd like to see your place, Pete."

That wasn't all he wanted to see. Once again, my horribly oversized cock had hooked a straight fish. I didn't know how it was going to work, but I didn't care. Nature finds a way.

By the time we walked from Venice to my place on Pico, the hot vibe had chilled a bit. Steve looked around like he was having second thoughts.

I watched his eyes dart about. "Steve, are you cool?"

Steve nodded. His mustache turned up as he smiled. "I'm just so fucking nervous. I've never done it with a guy like you."

That put my mind at ease. He'd done it with other guys. "I'll always be the biggest, but how big was the previous record holder?"

Steve concentrated. "Some Austrian asshole. Thinks he owns the place. I can't stand his personality. But fuck! He wasn't hung like a horse, but it was damn big."

I winced a little at the implied accusation. I was hung like a horse. Stomp! Whinny! But he didn't mean it that way.

"What's the smallest you've ever been with, Pete?"

I shrugged. "Three inches, maybe."

"I got him beat by an inch, at least." Steve blushed. He was an outwardly proud and confident man, but this was his Achilles heel. He was ashamed.

It was time for me to say what I had wanted to say back at the gym. "I love them small. The smaller, the better. I love when the whole package fits in my mouth. And little ones always cum so much more."

Steve smiled. "I didn't know there were people out there like you. My wife says I'm useless."

As we stepped over the threshold to my apartment, I put a firm hand on Steve's ass. "I like the whole package. Your ass is a monument to the male form."

Steve kissed me very suddenly. He put a hand down the front of my pants and put his hand on the root of my rapidly expanding cock. He undid my belt buckle, letting my chinos fall around my ankles. No underwear could contain me, so I was fully exposed.

I kneeled, unbuttoning Steve, exposing his tiny package. I put my mouth over it like a mother's nipple. I flicked his clit-like penis with my tongue.

He moaned. "Pete, not too fast. I cum quickly."

"And often, I hope?"

He laughed. "Yeah, I got a few loads in me. You'll see."

And I did. It took less than a minute for Steve to shudder and release a flood of cum in my mouth. I gulped it down like milk. Steve threw his head from side to side, sucking air and grunting.

After another minute, the orgasm ended. Steve's shallow breaths returned to normal. He grinned. "Okay, my turn." He bent over, spreading his ass cheeks, revealing a pink squirming hole. I moved him to the sofa.

I did my best to hide my skepticism. Unless he were really experienced, he wouldn't even get the head in. I kept a tub of Albolene in the telephone table drawer. Steve took a big glob and applied it generously around and inside his hole. Meanwhile, I spread several generous helpings along the length and girth of my manhood.

"Steve, are you sure you want this? It's going to hurt."

"Dude, I'm a bodybuilder. I live for the burn."

Not surprisingly, when I put my head at the entryway, it wouldn't go any further. Steve pulled apart his ass cheeks to show a sliver of darkness in the middle of his pink pucker. That was my guide.

"Fuck me, Pete. I can take it."

He flexed his hole open wider, allowing the tip of my head to enter. I pushed gently but could go no farther.

"Pete, I mean it. Fuck me hard! Put it in me!"

I felt a rush of joy come over me. This man was my ideal lover. He wanted to please me, and he let me please him. To anchor his ass in place, I held him by the crotch. I could feel dribbles of precum forming rivulets in my hand. It made me even harder. Steve screamed.

"Oh god, I've hurt you!"

"No. You got really big for a second, but it's good now. Just keep pushing hard."

With an audible pop, I heard my head pass his inner sphincter. Even though my cock gets thicker all the way to the base, it still felt like a milestone. I got another six inches inside him before I hit the back of his rectum. I turned him on his side and pushed deeper, entering the colon.

Steve's eyes fluttered in his head. "Oh fuck man, I'm gonna fucking pass out." And he did. When he came to a few moments later, I was most of the way in. I had only about six inches to go. Steve wrapped his powerful legs around my waist and forced me all the way in. His eyes were fogged over from pure pleasure. He pushed me back with his feet, then pulled me in.

He did this a few times, establishing a rhythm. "Okay, Pete, you're in charge now."

He pulled off his t-shirt, revealing a powerful sweaty back and huge pectoral muscles dappled with fur. I got super hard, and he winced.

"Oh yeah. Don't hold back. Fuck my ass."

I thrust in and out with an ever-increasing speed. When I knew he could take it, I pulled the head of my cock right back to the entrance, then thrust it all the way inside his colon. The effect on Steve was extreme. He couldn't use words anymore, just guttural noises. Looking into his eyes, I could see a distant galaxy. His lips moved in time with my jackrabbit-paced fucking.

Steve's tiny dick was almost gushing precum. The clear sticky goo soiled the suede cushions of my couch. I didn't care. My cock was buried entirely inside this muscle god, and then it was almost out, then all the way in again, over and over. I had been with some talented bottoms, but none let me fuck them this deep or this fast. Steve was the best fuck of my life.

I could see Steve was about to cum hands-free. I rotated him so his cock faced me. I opened my mouth and caught the first massive load. I got the second and third spurts, too, then it shot all over my legs. It was so warm; I thought for a second he had pissed himself. I'd seen it happen plenty of times before, especially if I fucked hard and fast. Sure enough, after the cum came a fountain of piss, ruining my couch. It was worth it.

The sense of power I felt at making another man cum and piss against his will was overwhelming. I felt a tingling in my balls that meant things were coming to their conclusion, at least for the moment.

"Steve, I'm gonna cum."

Steve's mouth hung agape, but he nodded. Only a moan escaped his lips.

I reached the zenith of my speed and ferocity. Steve started punching the arm of the couch. He broke it with his powerful arms and rock-hard fist. His huge glute muscles clamped around my cock like a vise. The added pressure was the tipping point. With my cock somewhere in his lower digestive tract, I fired round after round of cum inside the sexy bodybuilder.

With straight guys, I never kissed. But Steve pulled me close and rubbed his mustache against my lips. I had to break my rule. We locked tongues, exploring each other's mouths. I enjoyed the sensation of his mustache tickling the hairs of my nose. He tasted like cigarettes and testosterone.

We remained in that embrace for a long time. My cock softened, but it was too thick for Steve to push it out on his own. As long as I stayed wrapped in his arms, I was buried inside him. At last, he let go, and I stood up. Slowly, the mass of my cock came dislodged and exited Steve's asshole, followed by an obscene river of cum.

Steve came out of his reverie. "Oh shit, did I say anything stupid?"

"No, you didn't say anything at all."

Steve frowned. "Darn. I hoped I said something stupid like 'I love you.'"

He left his shrew of a wife and moved in with me. He couldn't afford to replace the sofa, so I made him work it off. His ass was so loose that his farts came out like a whisper.

❧ III ❦
COACHED

by Chuck Idgaf

LUKE'S COACH

Luke never really liked "boy" stuff. He preferred books...indoors. "Nerd" wouldn't be an inappropriate word. Growing up outside of town, he was raised in what most city folk would call "rural," but it wasn't really what most folks who know better would call "country livin'." They had chickens and a large garden. This meant Luke had plenty of chores, which he hated. It wasn't a bad childhood, but his family wasn't prone to showing affection or giving out compliments and words of encouragement. Luke was good at school, and his pleasant disposition made it easy for him to make friends. He saw how other families hugged and laughed. He couldn't say anything bad about his home life, but he did have a tinge of jealousy that he didn't have what some of his friends had.

Despite being more mathlete than athlete, his best friend somehow talked him into trying out for wrestling when he entered junior high. Lo and behold, he was a natural. Luke looked like a scrawny kid, but he was wiry. The chores he hated were paying off. Barely in the lowest weight class, he made quick work of his opponents in practice. He even bested some of his teammates in higher weight classes.

Luke liked that Coach. He wasn't aggressively macho. It was about the sport and sportsmanship, not ego. Coach always gave him compliments. He was proud that Coach thought he was one of the best on the team, even with him being one of the smallest. He felt a bond with Coach that he didn't have with his family. It gave Luke a welcoming, supportive environment to develop as he entered his teenage years.

Luke was a late bloomer. Puberty hit his last year in junior high. Just the touch of the sleek, tight fabric of his singlet made it difficult enough to keep hormones under control. He began to wear a protective cup in a jockstrap to help hide it. But it was painful to wear during matches and barely hid his noticeable excitement. He told Coach he needed to quit the team. Coach was not happy. Coach grilled him a while about why, and Luke finally said he was uncomfortable. Coach's angry face softened; he asked Luke if it made him aroused. Luke sheepishly nodded, his eyes welling up.

Coach sat next to him, "It happens to all of us. I'm sure you've noticed some of your teammates. It happens. Concentrate on the match. It will be fine."

Luke wiped his eyes with the back of his hand. "I can't," he said. Luke had figured out by this point that he was "different" from the other boys. He always knew he liked the shower room, but now he understood why. He thought maybe Coach knew he was different, too.

Coach said, "I hate to lose you, but I understand." Coach stood and stuck out his hand. Luke took it for a departing shake. He was grateful Coach didn't have any animosity towards him.

2

A COLLEGE TOUR

Jump forward a few years. Luke's a senior in high school. He has good grades, is an honor student, and is a member of some student clubs. Good enough to get some small scholarships but not enough to cover the big state school. They'll cover some of the cost of a community college, though.

He's touring the school campus he's most likely to attend...furthest from home. Tuition is mostly covered, and he's approved for work-study but hasn't been hired for a specific campus job yet. The dorms are an expense he'll have to figure out if he doesn't want to live at home and go to a closer school. Hopefully, work-study will cover that. Also, he didn't realize how expensive books were for college.

He's walking through the quad where all the student activities and organizations have booths set up for the visiting students. From behind him, he hears a questioning voice, "Luke?"

He turns to see Coach. Through their conversation, he learns that Coach now works for the college, and their wrestling team won the state championship last year. Coach asks about his scholarships, nodding while listening.

When Luke finishes, Coach says, "Have you

thought about wrestling again? You look like you're still in great shape for it." Luke's cock twitches at the thought of wearing a singlet again. Coach says, "I can possibly get you a partial scholarship, given your winning record in junior high. It would probably cover the rest of your expenses, and then your work-study would be spending money."

Luke mulls it over while finishing his tour. He really likes the school and knows this is too good an opportunity to let his worries from junior high hold him back. "Besides," he thinks, "I'm an adult now. Surely I can control my erection more than during puberty."

He goes back to the booth and accepts Coach's offer. There's a few weeks of paperwork back and forth, but it's all done before his high school graduation. Coach has Luke on a training routine over the summer to get ready for the next semester. Luke is excited about school, and wrestling again.

*

Luke's having trouble getting to sleep. First night in a new bed. Plus, his balls ache to be drained. Tom is asleep. Not snoring, but clearly out like a light. Luke pulls down his briefs and begins to stroke as quietly as he can, but the bed creaks when he makes too much movement. He's finally got a good slow rhythm going, and Tom switches sides. Luke freezes, waiting to make sure he hasn't woken up. Luke realizes this won't be productive, so he grabs his towel and heads to the showers.

To his surprise, he can hear a shower running as he gets near. As he enters the bathroom, he can tell by the broad shoulders and fuzzy back in the middle stall that it's Mike. He's not sure by the arm motion if Mike is lathering up or jerking off. Luke lets the door close, making its telltale noise. Mike leans back and looks as Luke nods hello. Mike looks a little sheepish, "Uh. I'm taking care of a little business...I hope that's ok."

Luke, in a rare moment of not being his normal, re-served self on such matters, says, "From the brief glimpse earlier, there's nothing little about it."

Mike makes a hearty laugh. As he laughs, he turns. Luke's eyes go wide involuntarily at the sight of Mike's cock. It's the size of a tall boy beer can. Mike holds it by the base and shakes it at Luke. "I like you, kid; you're funny." Luke laughs back, trying to recover from the sight. Mike asks, "You're cool if I finish, right?" as he turns back into his shower stall.

Luke swallows hard. Mike obviously has a ton of self-confidence. This empowers Luke a little, and he decides to be candid. "I'm...kind of here for the same reason." Mike says from behind the wall, "Cool, man. We all do it. I don't get why some guys are so embarrassed. Better out than in, I say."

Luke feels bolder now. He takes the stall next to Mike. He begins to stroke. Luke has a very average cut cock, but veiny and hard as steel. His eyes are closed. He plays with his nipples, then tugs his balls while stroking. He can hear the fapping noises Mike is making. This makes it hotter. Luke's got a good rhythm going, lost in the sensation. He doesn't notice the change in the sound of water hitting the floor in Mike's stall. He jumps as Mike says from right behind him, "Let's see what you're working with, buddy?"

Luke freezes. Does Mike know he's into guys? Is this a trick? Or hazing? Luke turns slightly, looking like a deer in headlights. Mike says, "Oh. Sorry, buddy. Didn't mean to freak you out. Have you never circle-jerked with your buds before?" Luke shook his head no, still wide-eyed." Mike, "My bad. Sorry. (awkward pause) Is that something you'd be cool with?" Luke swallows, "I...guess." "Cool," Mike smiles," Just buds having a good time."

Luke finishes turning towards Mike, cock standing straight out. Mike looks down, "Nice one, man. That's a good size." Luke half smiles at the compliment. Mike shakes his hard cock once, "Guys think it's great to have a big dick, but really it can be hard finding a girl willing to try. And forget about a blow job." Mike reaches out and squeezes Luke's cock. Luke tries not to jump at his touch. "Wow." Mike says, "That is rock hard. You could hammer a nail through a board with that thing. I'm at full mast, and mine's still kind of spongy, see." Mike thrusts forward, offering Luke a feel, still holding Luke's cock. Another awkward moment passes as neither moves.

Then slowly, Luke reaches out and squeezes. It's the first penis that wasn't his he's touched. He notices the sheer girth of it. The heft and weight. But then, yes... spongy. It's erect, firm even, but nothing like Luke's own. Mike strokes Luke. "Yeah, that's nice and hard. You could get into the tightest of holes with that thing." Luke slowly strokes Mike, noticing the skin sliding with his hand, not under. Back and forth. Longer strokes, now feeling the full length.

Mike says, "Yeah. That feels great. Would you be OK jerking each other off?"

Luke is speechless but nods. Mike closes his eyes, and each finds a nice rhythm to stroke the other.

After a few minutes, Luke is lost in bliss when Mike says, "I'm getting close. Would you finish me, then I'll finish you?" Luke doesn't really know what he means but says, "Sure."

Mike turns around, taking Luke's arm to show him how to reach around him. Luke sees how this is more comfortable, like jerking his own cock. He strokes faster as Mike breathes harder. Mike's really working his nipples. Luke's cock is pointing upward, wedged in Mike's crack. Mike is thrusting his hips, rubbing Luke's cock against him in the process. Luke is in heaven. The rubbing makes Luke jerk faster. Luke's hips and cock thrust on autopilot as Mike thrusts into his jerking fist.

Mike says he's going to cum. Luke squeezes a little more while jerking faster. He can feel the huge pulses through Mike's cock. His spunk splatters the wall across from them—one spurt after another. Luke can't believe someone can produce so much spunk. He slows his motions as the volleys come to an end; he lets go and gently backs away from Mike.

Mike finally recovers and turns around. "Damn, buddy. That was incredible."

Luke smiles with pride. "Not a bad first time jerking off someone else," he thinks to himself.

Mike's still semi-hard, oozing the last of his load. "Now it's your turn," Mike says with a devilish grin. He motions for Luke to turn and face the shower. Mike wraps his big arms around Luke. One hand on his cock, the other tugging his balls. He begins to stroke. Luke can feel Mike's fat cock running down his crack, like a fat hotdog on top of a too-tiny bun. Mike's stroke is excellent, just grazing Luke's tightly cut cock.

Mike whispers in his ear, "That's a great cock, buddy. So firm. Great for stroking." His words drive Luke closer to the edge. He can feel Mike's cock start to get hard again, rising into his crack. He can feel his nuts begin to draw up as he gets closer. Mike tightens his finger and thumb around Luke's sack and tugs gently, keeping his nuts from tightening. The sensation is incredible. Mike seems to be an expert and jerking. Luke hopes to learn more from him but, for now, gets lost in the sensations.

Mike is harder still, knowing he's getting Luke close. Mike's fat cock head grazes Luke's hole. That's all it takes. Luke's whole body spasms. Mike says in his ear, " Yeah, buddy. Shoot that spunk for me. Drain those balls." As Luke begins to cum, Mike lets go of his balls, letting them draw up and shoot all they contain. Luke nearly collapses as his orgasm subsides.

Mike says, "Man, that load was almost as big as

mine." Luke smiles. Mike goes back to his shower to rinse and finish up. They say their good nights and return to their rooms. Luke falls asleep almost instantly.

*

Early morning the next day for workout and first practice. A majority of the team are new freshmen; he met most of them at dinner last night. They divide up based on weight class. Luke manages to "shake the rust off" pretty quickly, just like when he was younger. He realizes he really is a natural at the sport. Even though he hasn't actively wrestled in years, he manages to keep up with, if not best, his teammates. Luke also likes the way his singlet feels. Like an old blanket. But he's also glad he got drained so thoroughly last night because the way it rubs him also feels a little sensual.

Coach gives pointers and tips during various matches. Luke is making mental notes about his teammates' moves. His new roomie, Tom, is also quite good. He hasn't been pinned yet. Coach has been pairing some matches where someone in a lower class is up against someone with a weight advantage. Tom has a stalemate in one of these matches. Luke is impressed.

It's getting close to time to break for lunch, and Coach says, "Last match...calling Tom and Luke to the mat."

Tom has the advantage on nearly every front, but Luke manages to keep him at bay. Even though he's in the moment, concentrating on winning, he still manages to notice when their cocks touch, rubbing together as they struggle. Or when a hand near the balls pulls a thigh to pin the opponent. Luke is starting to tire. Tom's got him in a difficult hold. Luke, on instinct, remembers a move he used to pull when he was younger, twisting himself free and using Tom's own weight against him to get him off balance. Luke's got him pinned; now, to just hold him for the count. Tom's scent. It's stronger now. Luke ignores it, stays in the moment. Coach calls it for Luke. Everyone cheers.

Tom looks a little miffed as he gets up but gives Luke a hand to get up from the mat. Luke thinks he may have insulted Tom because he won't look him in the face. But then he realizes that Tom is looking at his crotch. Luke looks down. Not only is he raging hard, but has a big wet spot to boot. Tom just says, "Good match." as he walks toward the showers. Luke is mortified. He trudges dejectedly towards the shower room. Not only couldn't he control it, but he didn't even notice it was happening. What will he do during a match? "At least everyone else was walking toward the showers; I don't think they saw," he thinks, "Will Tom tell everyone?" As Luke looks up, he realizes someone else did see. Coach.

"You want to talk, kid?"

Luke shrugs an affirmative, and he changes course into Coach's office.

"Your worst fear, huh?" Coach says. Luke just nods, not looking up to avoid eye contact. "Look, son. It happens to all of us. Myself included. You can't control it all the time. It's a natural response for a lot of guys. You'll see. It'll happen to others on the team. You won't be the only one. We all just ignore it and walk it off." Coach puts a gentle hand on Luke's shoulder. He'd forgotten how Coach can make everything feel ok.

The weight of embarrassment lightens. Luke looks up and says, "Thanks, Coach."

"Anytime sport. Now go shower; you stink." They both laugh.

*

Luke wants to try to catch Tom alone, partially because of besting him on the mat but also to somehow play down the erection he got. But there are too many people around during lunch. And Luke has to rush across campus for a meeting about his work-study job.

Because of his class and practice schedule and his familiarity with the gym facilities from being on an athletic team, they offer him an evening job at the campus gym. Like most community colleges, this one is in a smaller town. The school lets local alumni have a membership in the evenings to help offset the cost, and students can also get access. His duties include resetting weight equipment when people don't put it back, laundry, restocking towels, and sweeping and mopping the locker rooms. Basic stuff. His orientation takes way longer than expected, and he has just enough time for a quick dinner before starting his first shift that evening.

Just as his job was described, he checks people in at the desk and returns dumbbells and barbells to the racks because of the inconsiderate lifters.

He folds and restocks towels. Each locker room has a sauna and steam room, so they go through plenty. He gets quite an eye full in the locker with some older locals. Who knew balls could be that saggy? He glimpses his first uncut cock while the guys towel off in the shower. He wasn't sure, but he could have sworn two middle-aged guys were up to something in the steam room, but the glass door was too foggy to be sure.

Fortunately, the gym closes at 8:00 pm. Plus, he only had to work a few days each week. The locker room views might end up being a bonus he hadn't expected.

As Luke enters the room, Tom is on the bed in a different-colored pair of briefs. "Where have you been?"

"I started work study today."

"Cool."

Luke shoe-gazes, "About today..."

Tom says, "That was some move." Luke looks up. Tom is smiling ear to ear. Luke's tension eases. "You're gonna have to teach me how to get out of a hold like that." Tom gets off the bed walking toward him, hand up for a high-five. Luke responds in kind, smiling. As the high-five passes, Tom goes in for a hug. Luke isn't prepared but quickly responds by hugging back. He can feel Tom's cock right next to his; Luke is rapidly hardening.

Tom says, "Glad you're on our team," and squeezes a little before ending the hug.

Luke's pants are tenting. Luke looks down, red with embarrassment again. Luke looks up to see Tom looking at his tent pole.

"Don't worry about that either," Tom says, "happens to me all the time."

Luke now notices that Tom's cock is rising but constrained in his briefs. Tom steps closer and says softly, "I didn't just mean on the wrestling team." Tom gently wraps his hand around the back of Luke's head, pulling him in for a kiss. Luke's mouth moves on instinct to accept. His first kiss. Perfection. Some tongue, not too much. Not too wet or dry. It feels in slow motion and forever.

Luke's arms are by his side, not that he notices. Tom grabs one and pulls it around his back. Luke follows with the other. Tom moves the one he's holding down toward his ass. Luke squeezes his taught bubble butt while thrusting his tongue deeper into Tom's mouth. The kiss becomes more frantic, passionate. Tom lifts Luke's shirt over his head. Luke removes his shorts. They kiss again, their brief-covered cocks rubbing against each other. Luke reaches down to point his upward to be more comfortable, the head just peering above the waistband.

Tom looks down to see. He uses his thumb to wipe a large drool of pre-cum from Luke's cock, then licks it from his finger. Luke swallows hard, his mouth suddenly dry. Tom adjusts himself the same way while Luke watches. But Tom shows an inch of shaft plus the head above the waistband. Luke rubs Tom's chest hair as they kiss, Tom guiding them to the bed.

They hump and frottage, lying on the bed. Luke

doesn't want the kissing to end. Tom has other plans. He nibbles his way down Luke's neck to his nipple and lightly bites. Luke gasps in pleasure. Not only from the nipple play but Tom's treasure trail against his exposed cock head. Tom works his way down, removing Luke's briefs. In one slow movement, Tom engulfs Luke's cock in his warm mouth, all the way nose to bush. Luke's eyes roll back in his head. He never imagined it would feel this incredible.

Tom works his tongue like a whirlwind while slowly bobbing. He reaches up and gently twists both nips. Luke wants it to last, but he can't hold out. He begins to cum. Tom swallows every spurt. Luke loses count of how many shots he makes, but it's more than he's ever done before. Tom keeps Luke's cock in his mouth until every last drop has oozed out. Tom crawls up and kisses him. Luke has tasted his own cum before, but it tastes even better in Tom's mouth as they kiss. Luke likes the kissing but wants to taste his first cock more. He's not subtle. He flips Tom off of him onto his back and quickly strips him of his briefs.

Tom's cock is a beauty. Luke's is around 6 inches. Tom's has to be 7 inches or a little more. It's slightly slimmer than Luke's but not thin by any means. He's got a thick bush too. There's a nice little dribble of pre-cum. Luke uses his tongue to lap it up. He loves the taste and the slickness of it. He repeats what Tom did, slowly working his way down. The sensation is incredible. Luke is instantly hard again with Tom in his mouth. He tries to go all the way to the bottom like Tom did but starts to gag. Tom gently tells him, "You don't have to take it all." Luke nods, most of it still in his mouth. He slowly moves up and down the shaft. Tom whispers, "Swirl your tongue." Luke complies. Tom moans loudly, his cock flexing in Luke's mouth. Luke can taste another drop of precum.

He understands now. More tongue, less bobbing. He

works his tongue in a circle just under the head. Tom moans, "Yes, that's the spot." Luke varies the motions of his tongue, testing what makes Tom's cock flex. Tom says, "You're a natural," as he runs his fingers through Luke's hair. Tom starts to thrust his cock in and out of Luke's mouth. Slow, shallow thrusts. Luke reaches up to play with Tom's nipples. He gives them a tweak, and Tom thrusts deeper while moaning, "Harder, baby." Luke pinches them. Tom thrusts faster. "Yeah, baby. Work my nips." Luke works his tongue as fast as he can while twisting and pulling Tom's nips.

Tom's hips buck wildly. "Fuck. Yeah. Here it comes." Tom's load unleashes in Luke's mouth. Luke swallows the first volley, but the second and third come too quickly. It's more than he can swallow; it oozes out around the shaft. Tom holds his head, thrusting.

Luke does his best not to gag. "At least he isn't thrusting too deep," he thinks. Tom slows and lets go of Luke's head. Luke pulls off Tom's cock and swallows, then laps up what's on his shaft and head. He realizes he loves the taste. Much better than his own. Tom pulls Luke up on top of him to kiss him deeply. Then he licks some of his own cum on Luke's chin to help clean him up.

"That was your first time, wasn't it?" Tom asks.

"Was it that bad?"

"Quite the opposite. You did really well for a first time. But I'll work on teaching you how to swallow big loads," Tom winks.

Luke smiles at him, and they kiss some more. They drift off to sleep in each other's arms.

*

Luke is working his fourth shift for the week in the gym. He's been working every evening with Melissa, another student. She's been working at the gym since last fall semester. She tells him, "Enjoy this slow week; it can get busy once students are back."

She helps Luke learn all the "shortcuts" to make the job easier to handle. He's gotten the routine down pretty well for the week. Folding towels fresh from the laundry seems never-ending. They take turns manning the front desk every fifteen minutes to walk the floor, ensure weights are put back correctly, and that machines look cleaned off. Every hour they each go check their respective locker room. Pick up towels. Wipe down sinks. Replace empty TP rolls. Check that the sauna and steam room are functioning and for lost items or left towels. Luke notices some guests are quite sloppy, leaving towels on the floor, even in the steam room. Someone has left a bottle of liniment in the steam room, which now smells of menthol and eucalyptus. He collects the occasional pair of swim trunks left behind on a hook after the person showered.

It's Luke's last walk-through of the night, just before closing. No one is in the locker room, so he sweeps near the lockers, mops quickly near the steam room and showers, picks up towels, and gathers the trash. As he returns from dropping the used towels in the laundry room, he notices a pair of skimpy red Speedos on a hook. He guessed he'd been looking at the floor for towels and didn't notice it before. He finishes his routine in the shower area by stretching out each stall's curtain to dry out.

As he finishes, he hears a noise in the steam room. As he opened the door, a blast of steam hit him in the face making it hard to see, but he could see enough. A man stood in the middle, his back to the door. He was middle-aged, fit, with dark hair and a Speedo tan line. As the steam cleared slightly, He realized there was another man in front of that man...bent over bracing on the bench in the steam room, swim trunks around his ankles. From what little he could see around the first man, the second was fair-skinned, a bit thicker build, and enjoying getting pounded in the ass. Although it felt like minutes in slow motion as Luke's eyes absorbed as much as they could, it was mere seconds. Luke's knee-jerk reaction was to awkwardly say, "Uhhhh, ten minutes 'til closing," while shutting the door and walking out of the locker room red-faced. Fortunately, Melissa was across the gym wiping down machines before she went to do the women's locker room, so he didn't have to explain his flush cheeks.

A few minutes later, the fair-skinned man left the locker room. Even though he'd obviously showered quickly, he was still red-faced and sweaty from the steam room exposure. Luke thought, "And maybe from getting off as well." He was stockier than Luke could tell earlier, maybe 40ish, with sandy brown hair. He had a cute, round, clean-shaven face that made him look younger, and kind eyes. Because he failed to button his shirt all the way up in haste, the gap exposes the soft, brown fur covering the man's chest. The man sheepishly nods hello at Luke as he hands over the locker key to get his car keys back. Luke smiles and gently nods back with a half wink, hoping the man understands, "Your secret is safe." Luke can see the man's shoulder relax a bit as he turns toward the exit. Luke watches the man exit, thinking how he can't wait to tell Tom.

He jumps as someone says, "Evening, Luke." Luke hadn't realized that the other man had exited the locker room. He also didn't know the other man was Coach.

"Evening, Coach," Luke says as he takes his locker key to the peg board. "Have a good workout?"

"Best I've had in a long time." Coach pauses. "I don't get the opportunity to exercise how I'd like."

Luke understands. "I can imagine that with a schedule like yours, it would be difficult to find time to fit in. And I'm sure there are limitations to the kinds of exercise you can do around here."

Coach smiles. His face is the same understanding face that had made Luke comfortable so many times before, but this time it shows that he appreciates being understood.

"See you at practice tomorrow. Get some rest," Coach says as he exits the gym.

*

"You'll never believe what happened at the gym tonight," Luke says, bursting into the dorm room. Tom is naked on his bed, reading a comic. Luke just stares at his beautiful cock. Eventually, Tom asks, "And? What happened." Luke snaps out of it and repeats the story.

"And then I turn around, and it was Coach!" Luke is incredulous.

Tom just laughs. "My gaydar always pinged a little with Coach, but sounds like he might be into bears."

"Bears?" Luke asks.

"Bigger guys, body hair, beards. You know."

Luke ponders. That makes Mike a bear. He did think the man was cute, also. "Hmm, that's something to explore," he thinks to himself.

"I only saw a few seconds, but Coach was really pounding him good. If I'd known it was Coach, I would have tried to get a better look."

Tom just winks as he laughs and leans in for a kiss. Tom is hard from hearing the story; his precum dribbles on the back of Luke's hand as they kiss. Luke was already rock hard, but now it's pulsing on its own against his shorts. He pulls away to undress.

"Have you ever done butt stuff?" Luke asks.

"Sure." Tom replies, "Fingering, prostate massage, top, bottom."

Luke, now naked, stands there looking a bit bewildered. He figured Tom would be more experienced than himself. He's guessing he may have underestimated. After a pause, he asks, "Will you teach me?"

"Sure. Where do you want to start?"

Luke thinks for a minute. "Fingering sounds like a good start. What's prostate massage?"

"Oh ho ho," Tom comically evil laughs, "you'll see."

Tom drags his mattress to the floor between their beds since the frames in the dorm squeak so much. He lays down a towel and gets some lube from his drawer. He has Luke lie on his stomach. "Now it's important to relax. Just take a deep breath in, then relax on the exhale. If something hurts, say so." Tom squirts lube on his fingers and rubs some on Luke's hole. Luke breathes in sharply at the wonderful sensation. Tom gently rubs his hole and applies a little bit of pressure. "Breathe in and hold." Luke does as he's told. "Now relax as you exhale." As Luke breathes out, his whole body, including his hole, relaxes a little. The bit of pressure Tom is applying lets his finger slip right into the second knuckle. Luke sighs at the pleasurable sensation. Tom dribbles a little more lube on Luke's crack, letting it run down to his finger. Tom works this lube into Luke's hole to make sure he has enough in there. Luke squirms in pleasure as the finger goes in and out. "Another breath," Tom says.

As Luke exhales, Tom's finger goes all the way in. Luke moans loudly. He feels Tom wiggle his finger a bit, and then a wave of euphoria rushes over him. Tom expertly applies pressure to Luke's prostate.

Luke involuntarily makes an "Ohhhh," rising in pitch as it draws on with each pulse Tom makes with his finger. "That, my boy, is prostate massage." Luke only barely hears him, his eyes rolling back into his head. Tom slides his finger in and out a few times, switching from the forefinger to the middle to get deeper. With his middle finger all the way in, he applies some pressure to Luke's hole: North, South, East, West. Loosening it. Stretching it. Tom pulls his finger out and stacks the middle finger on top of the forefinger. He gets the two tips in easily.

"Breathe again. Relax," he tells Luke. This time, as Luke exhales, Tom gets both fingers in up to the second knuckle. Luke makes a lower "Oh" sound.

"You good?" Tom asks.

"Oh, yeah," Luke replies.

Tom gently rotates from horizontal to vertical. Luke moans loudly. "Let's try something different."

Tom gets Luke on all fours, covers his cock with plenty of lube, and lines it up with Luke's hole. He applies just enough pressure to hold his cock's aim. Even after the two fingers, Luke's hole is still tight. "Now, as you breathe out this time, you push back into me at your own pace. You're in control," Tom says.

Luke breathes in, then out, but doesn't move. One more breath in. "Relax," he thinks. He loosens his shoulders and exhales, letting go of tension in the rest of his body. He pushes back, there's a little pressure, but he focuses on relaxing. And just like that, Tom's cock head gently slides past his tight little pucker. Luke gasps in ecstasy as he backs all the way, feeling Tom's bush on his ass checks. It's not completely comfortable, but the pleasure outweighs the pain.

"Congrats, Luke. You just lost your cherry." Tom spanks him playfully on the ass cheek. Luke moves forward and backward a few times slowly. He gets why so many men love it, but his freshly deflowered hole can't really take the friction of thrusting yet.

He tells Tom, "I understand."

"I wanted your first test run to be gentle," Tom says, gently pulling out. "Now it's my turn." He plops down on the mattress next to Luke.

Luke follows the same steps of loosening Tom's hole. He finds his prostate. Tom gives him instructions on how to apply pressure for pleasure. Luke notices Tom is good at relaxing, and it's easy for him to slip in two fingers.

Tom says, "I'm ready," as he rolls over onto his back. Luke looks a little confused as Tom pulls his legs up into the air. Tom smirks, "I want to see your face when you cum in me. It's your first fuck, after all."

Luke grabs Tom's ankles. Tom helps line up Luke's cock head to his hole. "When I breathe out, slowly push in," Tom says. Luke tries to be gentle. Tom relaxes with his breath, and Luke slides right in. It's so tight and so warm. He's all the way in but not sure what to do. Tom looks him in the eyes. "Fuck me."

Luke begins to thrust. Tom starts jerking his cock. Tom moans, giving Luke the confidence he needs. He takes longer thrusts. "Yeah. Fuck me harder." Luke thrusts harder. Tom moans louder with each thrust. The lust takes over Luke. He begins to thrust like a wild man, an animal. He grunts with every thrust. His balls tighten.

He whispers, "I'm gonna cum. I'm gonna cum. I'm gonna cum."

Tom moans. "Shoot it in me. Fill me with your spunk."

Luke takes a powerful thrust, the full length of his shaft, and then stops, buried deep in Tom. He feels Tom's hole squeeze and pulse against his shaft. Tom is cumming spurt after spurt on his chest as Luke cums deep in his ass. After the first few volleys, Luke begins to thrust again, trying to extend his orgasm. Tom moans, "Yes. Yes. Harder." Luke obeys. Tom has another orgasm, this time covering his face and the wall behind him.

Luke's own orgasm subsides, and he pulls out and falls on the mattress next to Tom. After they catch their breath, Tom says, "Next time, I'm gonna fill up your tight hole."

Luke replies, "I look forward to it."

They clean up the room and head to the shower to clean up before sleep.

*

Over the next couple of weeks, they suck each other off almost every night. As promised, Tom has filled Luke's hole with a substantial load a few times. The last time, Luke was on his back and managed to cum hands-free. Even Tom was impressed. Tom, of course, has returned the favor, letting Luke try doggie style, or cowboy style, with Tom riding him, just to give him the full experience.

Today is their first wrestling match. Luke is feeling good about it. Practice has been going well. He's competing as if he hadn't given it up for a few years. His match starts; they are both pretty evenly matched. He quickly gets his opponent in a hold from behind. The other guy manages to make his way out of it and get Luke into a hold. Luke gets out without much effort and flips into a hold where they are each facing outward. The boys squirm around to face each other, struggling to gain dominance in the match. Suddenly Luke feels a familiar feeling. A hard cock against his belly...his opponent's.

"Coach was right," he thinks. He's distracted, and the guy breaks free and pins Luke from behind. Luke can feel the erection rubbing between his ass cheeks. Luke can feel his own cock beginning to plump. The fear gives him a power boost. He breaks free. He gets the other guy pinned, but their cocks rub against each other as they struggle. The ref begins the count. Luke wins. They break apart.

The other guy offers a handshake. "Good match," he says. Luke is baffled. It's like he doesn't even know his boner is showing. He could care less.

It's all Luke can think about. He manages to say, "Thank you," as they shake hands. Luke hunches over in a failed attempt to hide his erection. Adding to his horror, he notices he has a huge wet spot visible. He sits watching the rest of his teammates' matches, trying not to make contact with anyone.

Coach comes up to him in the locker room. Most of the other guys are in the showers. "Great match today, champ."

"Thanks," he says in a down tone.

Coach puts a calming hand on Luke's shoulder. "You did notice the other guy, right? I told you it happens to everyone."

Luke looks around. Then softly, "But I had a giant wet spot, too!"

Coach laughs. "So? You're a leaker. You'll be grateful for that in other situations." Luke just shrugs.

Coach has his stern voice on now. "That guy didn't notice. And he was up close. I didn't see anyone pointing or staring. Everyone that likes this sport knows that it's natural, and it happens whether the person wants it to or not. I saw it when it caught you by surprise. But you managed to keep your head in the game and win—this time. Ignore your embarrassment. You're an athlete. Focus on the sport. Plus, that was a great match. Even that guy knew it. He acknowledged it with that handshake."

Luke knows Coach is right. But he still wishes he'd had better control.

Coach softens his voice now. "Remember how I... exercise?"

Luke looks up at him, puzzled as to where this is going.

"I'm sure you exercise daily." Pausing as he finds the words. "Even if you don't have a spotter, you probably exercise by yourself."

Luke nods, understanding the metaphor.

"Maybe you should exercise right before a match." Coach shrugs. "Just a thought."

Luke thinks Coach might be onto something.

The Gym has settled into a regular rhythm now that school is a few weeks into the semester. The initial rush of students has waned to just the regulars, and they usually finish by 6:00 or 6:30 so they can hit the cafeteria before closing. Luke also notices that few, if any, of the students use the locker rooms. They come in workout clothes and shower in the dorms. A few football players may come through and use the steam room after practice, but that's it.

During practice earlier that day, Luke landed hard on his shoulder. Coach had come in early to use some of the cardio machines. He asked Luke about his shoulder, and Luke said it was OK, but that was at the beginning of his shift. Now it is quite tender to move, making towel folding a slower task than usual.

Coach comes out of the locker room and notices Luke is struggling with the towels. "Are you sure about that shoulder, bud?"

Luke says, "It does hurt more than before." Coach walks into the gym office and returns with some over-the-counter pain relievers, anti-inflammatory pills. Nancy, the evening manager, follows Coach out.

She says, "Coach says you had a bad tumble earlier today."

Luke replies, "I just landed hard on the mat." He swallows the pills with water from the dispenser beside the front desk.

Coach says, "You might want to try the sauna. Help loosen those muscles. Then get a good night's sleep."

Nancy nods in agreement. "There's only an hour left before we close, Luke. Go ahead. There's only a few regulars left. We can finish towels tomorrow."

Luke says he appreciates it, grabs a locker key for his clothes, and says goodnight to Coach as they depart in different directions.

The sauna is a nice size and has an L-shaped bench with two levels. He doesn't bother turning on the light; plenty is coming through the glass door from the locker room. Since no one else is there, Luke lays out naked on a towel on one of the upper benches. He tries to relax his whole body. After a few minutes, he realizes Coach was right, and his shoulder doesn't hurt as bad as it did. He enjoys the dry heat. Getting comfortable, he's just about to doze off when the door opens. Luke looks up, not at the man, but to make sure he's not blocking all the bench space. Then he turns to the person walking in. The man is backlit, so he's unsure who it is, but Luke asks, "Do you want me to get up?" "No," the man replies in a kind voice, " there's plenty of room for me on the other bench."

Luke closes his eyes again as he lays back down. He can hear the man climb up and sit on the other upper bench. "I'm Rob, by the way."

"I'm Luke," he says before looking up and then realizing he recognizes the man. It's Coach's "friend" from a few weeks ago. Luke has seen him work out a few times since then and has always been polite, but noticed that his locker room time has been brief. The way the light is coming through the door, Luke can get a better look than he's been able to before. He's wearing his towel, but his legs are stocky and fuzzy, not overly hairy, but he thinks it makes them look manly. His chest and belly have soft brown short fur all over. He has a bit of a belly, not too big, and his chest is flabby. Luke finds it odd; he wants to hug the man. There's something teddy bearish about him. That also makes him attractive to Luke. Trying to defuse his awkwardness, Luke says, "Oh hi, yes, I've seen you in before. I must have missed you coming in to work out earlier."

Rob smiles, his cheeks a bit red, "I just got here to use the sauna. Rough day at work." Luke nods in understanding, then lays back down. He rotates his shoulder and arm in a bunch of directions. "Did you hurt something?" the man asks.

"Landed wrong in practice," Luke replies.

"Oh. Sorry to hear that. I do massage on the side. Would you like me to work on it a little?"

Luke sits up. "That would be great. Sure you don't mind?"

"Not at all."

Luke wraps his towel around his waist, "Nice to officially meet."

They shake hands, and Luke sits between Rob's legs on the lower bench. Rob goes to work.

Luke realizes how much it still hurts. To distract himself from the initial pain, he asks, "Massage on the side?"

Rob answers while he works, "Yes. I'm an accountant to pay the bills. I took a class in Massage back in college. Here, in fact. I really enjoyed the therapy aspect of it, but there's also a bit of Zen for me. I can zone out on the stress and baggage of my day job. I have a little studio in my home, but I don't have any regular clients. I have listings on a few sites, so I get to do it occasionally."

As Rob moves Luke's arm in different directions and applies pressure with his other hand, Luke notices the pain is already much better. "The heat in here is making the work go faster," Rob says as if he knew what Luke was thinking.

Rob works Luke's neck, shoulders, and upper back. Luke's never had a massage before, but he definitely wants to again. Luke's head is leaning forward while Rob works. Luke opens his eyes to see his full erection standing up between the ends of the towel. He tries to cover it.

Rob says, "That happens to most guys when they get this relaxed. Nothing to be ashamed of."

"Coach says the same thing," Luke mumbles.

"Coach is a smart guy. One of the best people I know."

Luke doesn't know what comes over him, but before he even realizes it, he asks, "Do you two know each other well?"

"Well, it IS a small town, so everyone knows everyone, but I'd say we're friends. We do get to spend some time together on occasion, but not often."

Luke swallows. "Do you have many friends here?"

Rob sighs, "Not really. The odd acquaintance or a friend who travels through once in a while."

Luke feels possessed like he can't control what he's saying. "Would you like me to be your friend?"

He can hear the smile in Rob's voice, "That is awfully kind of you, but most of my friends are usually a bit older than me."

"Oh," Luke sounds dejected, "that makes sense."

"Do you not have ANY friends of your own?" Rob asks.

"I do. But it's fairly new," Luke pauses, "I guess I'm just curious about different types of friends and the things they might do together. You know, how different people have different hobbies." Luke thinks to himself that he's getting really good at talking in code.

After a pause, Rob says thoughtfully, "Maybe you're just looking for a mentor."

Luke turns to look up at Rob. "Maybe you're right."

Rob says, "Speak plainly. Not doublespeak."

Luke stands up to face Rob and looks him in the eyes. His cock is sticking straight out from the towel still. Luke has never been so candid, "There's something about you. I can't decide if I want you to bear hug me or let me do what Coach did."

Rob's eyes widen, "Well. That is quite bold, young man," as he gets up, stepping down to floor level with Luke. Luke has to back up a little to give him room. Rob grabs Luke's cock with one hand and the back of his head with the other while going in for a kiss. Luke meets him halfway, their tongues swirling around each other. Luke's hands instinctively go to Rob's chest, rubbing his fur and working his nips. He can't believe how rubbing Rob's belly makes his cock flex. Rob pulls back, "You're in charge. Tell Daddy what you want, son."

Luke leans in, then softly but firmly says, "Bend over." Rob turns around and takes his towel off. Luke sees he has light fuzz on his back but thick fur on his ass cheeks. Rob folds the towel on the upper bench and leans on it with his elbows. Luke realizes he doesn't have any lube.

Rob can sense his hesitation, "Spit on it." Luke freezes. Rob more gently, "Spit a good loogie on my hole and the tip of your cock. Don't worry. Daddy can take it. I'm gonna mentor you in the old ways."

Luke spreads Rob's hairy cheeks and hocks a good one just above his pucker, letting it dribble down. Then another on his cock head. He lines up his cock to Rob's hole, and before he can do anything else, Rob slides all the way back. "Now pump me full of jizz, boy. I need a good fucking after the day I've had." Luke does as he says. He begins to thrust. Rob's hairy ass is driving him crazy. He's pulling out for full strokes and pushing in as hard as he can. Rob groans with each thrust. Luke's thrusts get shorter and faster as he gets closer to cumming.

"Yeah, boy. Fill my hole," Rob says as he starts to jerk his own cock, "That's it, boy. You're gonna make me cum with that hard cock." That sends Luke over the edge. One deep thrust and all his spunk fills Rob's hole. Luke can feel it oozing out around his cock and into his pubes. He's never felt a load that big before.

Rob is still jerking fast as a madman, "Leave it in, boy. Daddy's close." Luke reaches around and takes Rob's dick in his hand. It's barely 5 inches long, but there's a gap between his finger and thumb. By comparison, it makes Mike's dick feel normal-sized. It's like jerking a soup can. Rob grabs his nips, and Luke starts to thrust with his still-hard cock.

"Fuck yeah, son. Fuck the cum outta me." Luke jerks and fucks faster. Suddenly, Rob's hole clenches down on his cock. He can feel his prostate throb against his cock as the bench is doused in Rob's cum. They catch their breath. Rob uses his towel to clean the bench. Rob says, "I guess I should mentor some." He winks as Luke chuckles. "Spit is ok for those with enough experience. I get tested regularly, but you shouldn't be fucking strangers without condoms. You're a considerate lover. But sometimes, bottoms just want to get fucked. Other times, they want to get fucked to cum. And variations in between. Be clear with your communication. It can be better for everyone. Have a good one, kid."

"Thanks, Rob. I appreciate the insight...and every-thing else." Luke winks.

Luke gets back to the dorm room. Before Tom can say hello, Luke says, "I think I have a thing for bears..."

Tom's cock is already starting to harden, "Do tell. Exciting night at the gym?" Tom reaches for the lube, so he can stroke and enjoy the story he's about to hear.

*

Campus is pretty empty on Saturdays. Most students go home for the weekend. Tom has a car, so he and Luke decide to goof off in the next town over at their annual festival on the square. It's a nice day of fair food, kooky arts and crafts, mediocre rides, and some surprisingly decent live music. The boys finish the day with a movie at the cinema, which they had to them-selves because of the festival.

It's late when they get back to the dorm. All is quiet since it's mostly empty. On the way to their room, they can hear the water running in the dorm showers. Luke takes a quick peek, and sure enough, it's Mike. He gently closes the door. "I think Mike's about to have some alone time," Luke says with a devilish grin. "Should we join him?"

Tom doesn't answer; he just takes off, racing to their room. Luke catches up. Once inside, they both strip, slinging clothes everywhere, wrap their towels around their naked waists, and run back to the shower. Luke gently closes the door behind them. They quietly hang their towels on the hooks and then make their way over toward Mike. Mike is facing into the stall, his arm working a mile a minute.

"Having a good time?" Luke says.

Mike jumps as they caught him off guard. He turns, a bit in shock. Once he realizes it's Luke, he laughs. "Hey, buddy. Yeah, I'm enjoying it." Tom's jaw drops. He's seen Mike in the showers before, but never at full mast. "Tom, right?" Mike sticks out his hand for a shake. Tom shakes his hand, never breaking eye contact with his crotch.

Mike laughs, "This one is funny. Ya'll here for the same reason, I guess?"

Luke says, "You've guessed correctly," and laughs. Luke and Tom each turn on a shower on either side of Mike, rinse a bit, and turn to face each other, making three sides of a square to watch each other jerk. Luke is pretty sure Mike is turned on by Tom's attention to his big cock.

Mike stops wanking, looks at Tom, and motions to his cock. He says, "You want to give it a go?" Tom nods as he reaches out and begins to stroke Mike. Mike reaches over and takes Tom's cock in return. "That's a nice one, Tom. About as long as mine." Tom looks up for the first time and smiles at him. Mike takes his other hand, moving Luke's hand out of the way to stroke Luke also.

"It's like skiing," Mike says. They all laugh. After a bit, Mike looks at Luke, "You wanna give it a go again?"

Luke says, "I sure do." Luke and Tom swap hands on Mike's cock. Luke moves in front of him for a different angle. He kneels, and before Mike can say anything, Luke manages to get the head and several inches in his mouth.

"Whoa...Oh....OOOHHHH," Mike moans. It feels even thicker in Luke's mouth. He's proud he's managed to get this much in. He's really working his tongue around like Tom taught him. Mike gently rests his free hand on top of Luke's head. He closes his eyes and leans his head back. Tom reaches over to work his nipples while Mike continues to stroke him.

Mike finally says, "This is my first real blow job. It feels incredible." Luke works on Mike's cock a while longer, Mike moaning low the whole time.

Tom taps Luke on the shoulder, "My turn." They swap. Mike strokes Luke's cock now while Luke runs his fingers through Mike's furry chest. Luke's cock is so hard it almost hurts. He makes his way up and plays with Mike's beard. Even though it's soft and downy, it's handsome.

Luke starts to go in for a kiss. Mike senses it and opens his eyes. Mike whispers, "I really like the jerking, but that's all I'm interested in." He smiles at Luke. Luke gets the message and diverts his mouth to Mike's nipple. Mike growls and Luke nibbles on it; Mike puts his hand on Luke's head and tousles his hair. "Yeah, that's good," Mike growls at Luke.

Tom gets up, rubbing his knees from the hard tile. "Would you like to finish somewhere more comfortable? No funny stuff, we promise."

Mike says, "Sure."

They dry off and head back to their room. The boys get the mattress back on the floor. Mike lays down, and Luke crawls between his legs. Luke is leaking up a storm enjoying sucking Mike's thick cock, even though he can only get a little more than half in his mouth. Luke then thinks about Rob. He's even thicker. He hopes he gets a chance to test his skills on Rob one day. While lost in thought, he doesn't notice Tom has gotten the lube out. Luke feels a finger inserted into his hole. Luke moans as it slips in. He and Tom have experimented a bit more with each other and some toys. Luke has really learned to relax and enjoy.

Tom leans over Luke and whispers, "Are you ready

to finally get fucked properly?" Luke nods and moans an affirmative, never removing Mike's fat cock from his mouth. Tom aims his cock, and gently slides all the way in. Luke makes a grunt from the momentary sensation of being stretched open.

Mike opens his eyes. "Whoa...that's kind of hot." Mike grabs a pillow to prop his head up so he can watch Luke get spit roasted. With every slow thrust Tom makes, Luke becomes more insatiable on Mike's cock. Luke manages to get another inch or so of Mike's cock in his mouth. Tom picks up speed as he senses Luke loosening up. Mike holds Luke's head and makes little thrusts. Luke uses one hand on Mike's balls and another on a nipple. Mike growls with every twist. Tom is turned on by how much of Mike's cock Luke has gotten in his mouth, and watching Mike slowly, gently thrust. The site is sending him over the edge. Tom grabs Luke's hips and thrusts harder. Luke Moans with every thrust. Mike moves faster, careful not to choke him while working on the cum boiling up from his big balls. "I'm gonna cum, buddy."

Luke nods and moans in acceptance. Tom yells, "Fuck, yeah. Take that load, Luke. I'm gonna bury mine in your ass, too."

As if in sync. Tom and Mike both throw their heads back and moan loudly as they fill Luke from both ends. Luke's cock erupts without being touched. Mike's cum is so much that Luke can't swallow it all. It runs down his chin from around Mike's shaft. He can feel Tom's cum running down his balls as it leaks out while Tom continues to pound. Luke's own cock is still pulsing from his orgasm, even though he ran out of jizz after the sixth spurt. They begin to slow their collective thrusts as their orgasms subside.

As they both pull out, Luke collapses on his side. He's a cum-covered mess and never felt so satisfied. Mike is the first to speak. "Damn. That was incredible.

I didn't think I'd ever be able to get a blow job, let alone one that amazing. I like pussy when I can get it, but damn, you gay boys know how to suck a dick."

The boys laugh. Luke says, "Anytime you need a hand."

Tom adds, "Or mouth." They all laugh.

After Mike leaves, the boys go to rinse the sex off in the shower. Luke wipes off with a towel first, so he's not too suspicious if they run into someone in the hall. Luke says, "I wonder what it'd be like to get fucked by one that big."

Tom laughs, "Slow down, power bottom in the making." They both laugh. "Did you enjoy it tonight? Getting fucked?"

Luke looks incredulous, "Do you have to ask? I came without touching my dick."

Tom says, "I just thought that was from choking on Mike's fat cock."

Luke laughs. "That may have helped a little." They laugh again.

Tom says more seriously, "Big dicks require working up to it. You should also make sure it's a top that understands the pain and damage they could cause. Some guys are rough and don't care. Be careful when the opportunity finally comes around for a big one." Luke nods, understanding.

*

Luke has really enjoyed his first semester at college. He and Tom are best friends with benefits. Tom has taught him a lot, and Luke feels comfortable in his own skin for the first time in his life. Tom's helping him develop his gaydar. They hook up with two other students they'd met. Tom shows him the ropes on how and where to cruise. Second-floor library bathroom, where they met the first student (the second is in one of Tom's classes). The cross-country trails for meeting up and what signals to look for. The gym, of course, which is more difficult for Luke since he works there. They know about the dirty bookstore two towns over but have never explored it. Tom tells Luke he'd read online that the rest area off the interstate could be as well, but neither of them has braved it.

Most of Luke's limited experiences happen at the river. There's a sandbar in a small river not too far away where people like to hang out on weekends. Tom shows Luke the trails that lead upriver to a bank in a bend where people sunbathe nude and the cruising that happens further in the woods on the trails. This mostly leads to some jerk sessions, some of those while watching other men suck and fuck. A few BJs from a variety of ages, some much older. As winter approaches and the weather gets cooler, studies take over, and Luke's schedule becomes more class, study, practice, work, match.

*As the semester nears its end, the season's final match is here. The tournament is held at a large athletic center. The facilities are nice, with multiple locker rooms to accommodate such events. Most of his teammates have early matches. Luke is in line to rank 1st in the state in class, so his first match isn't in the first few rounds. He's feeling the pressure a bit before the match, knowing that winning might help him with scholarships for a four-year college.

Luke has been following Coach's suggestion of 'exercising' ("My right arm," Luke thinks to himself) right before each match. It's really helped him keep his unwanted public erections under control this season. He starts his routine in a bathroom stall, like usual. He always begins by rubbing his nipple through the material of his singlet until his dick is hard. The strain of the singlet against his cock feels wonderful. Eventually, he pulls his singlet to the side to access his cock and balls.

Getting hard, like always, is easy enough. Today, though, he is too distracted by the realities of the finals and can't seem to accomplish his goal of emptying his balls to get out to the mats. He hears Coach calling his name from the locker room. He realizes how long he's probably been in the stall. He can hear Coach right outside the stall, realizing that his shoes gave away his location.

"What's the problem, son?" Luke's cock throbs at Coach calling him son. He's always thought of Coach as a father figure. That's something new to process.

Luke says softly through the crank in the door. "I can't seem to finish, uh, 'exercising.' And been trying for a while. And it's definitely not going down," he finishes frantically.

"I feel sorry for you, kid. I truly sympathize. But what do you want me to do about it? You've got 15 minutes or so before the next round starts."

After a pause, Luke leans closer to the door. "Can you...can you help me?"

Coach chuckles, "I love you, kid, but I'm not risking my job for you."

In a higher-than-normal voice, Luke says, "What should I do?"

Coach looks around. The locker room is mostly empty, just the occasional person coming back for something they forgot. It's early in the tournament, so most people are out watching or participating on the floor. He turns back towards the door. "Make your way to the last stall. I'll see if I can get some help."

Luke wipes the precum from his tip before pulling his singlet back over his erection, not that it's hiding much, but he knows he can't walk out of the stall with his boner pointing straight out at anyone who might walk by. He walks down to the last stall, the farthest away from the door. He's not sure why Coach has sent him down to this stall, but he realizes he probably should have done that to begin with, just in case someone noticed what he was doing.

He begins to stroke again, removing his cock from his singlet so he doesn't get a wet spot. His eyes close, concentrating on the sensations his strokes give his cock. He's so close to cumming, but he just can't make it happen. He's jarred to his senses when he hears the stall door next to him shut and lock. He wonders who it is. The thought turns him on. He thinks about how Coach knew it was him in the stall by his feet. He tilts his head and sees black shower shoes. It could be any-one; the majority of his team has those same ones. It's likely that most people at the tournament do, too. "Even Coach has those kind," Luke begins to wonder but is interrupted by the feet as they turn and face to-wards him. Luke can hear some light scraping on the cubicle wall.

Luke doesn't know what to make of the situation. Just as he starts to wonder if he should worry, the toilet paper holder slides out of the way, revealing a hole be-tween the stalls. "Oh," Luke thinks, "this must be a glory hole. Tom told me about these, but I didn't think I'd ever see one. Especially in a place as fancy as this facility." Luke then realizes the TP holders are rigged together on both sides to hide it so it doesn't get re-paired. Luke wakes from his thoughts to discover that two fingers are tapping the bottom of the hole. Luke's not sure what that means. He hears the other person clear his throat and tap again slower. Luke realizes he's supposed to put his cock through. He puts it all the way through, his chest and belly flat to the wall, his head turned to the side. A warm mouth engulfs his cock. He stifles a moan. An expert tongue goes to work.

The oral skills of the cocksucker are exceptional, but Luke realizes the situation is making it even more erotic. Luke understands the stories he's learned over the last few months of the "days of old" cruising. Luke begins to thrust, his hands flat on the wall, wishing they could hold the back of the head sucking him. Luke can feel his balls finally starting to draw up, preparing to empty into a willing mouth. The guy on the other side of the wall notices, too, because he grabs Luke's balls and pulls down against their natural ascension. The sensation is just what Luke needs to push him over the edge. Luke bites his hand to muffle the scream of ecstasy as his load is finally purged. As the pulses subside, he feels a hand wrap around the base of his shaft to squeeze every last drop into the mouth still wrapped about his cock. Luke pulls his cock out of the hole. It's mostly limp already from the intense orgasm. He gets his cock and balls tucked in his singlet and leans towards the opening, whispering, "Thank you." He hears an affirmative "um hm" in response as he opens the door and runs towards the mats, hearing his name being called over the speakers for the next round.

*

Luke steps down from the podium, a 1st place state champion medal around his neck. Tom places 2nd in his class. Another guy from their team got 3rd in his. The whole team is hugging and patting each other on the back. They all make their way to the locker room to shower and change, ready for celebrations before the bus ride home. Luke is lagging behind, exhausted from the mental stresses of the day. The match and what happened before. A familiar, gentle hand lands on his shoulder, "I'm proud of you, son. You did great out there."

He looks up over his shoulder at Coach and smiles. Luke stands, "Thanks for everything, Coach."

"It was nothing. You put in all the work." Luke smiles, "That, too. But I meant earlier."

Coach blinks at him, "I didn't do anything." Coach pauses, realizing it's not registering. "I just told you to be at the right place and hoped for the best."

Luke's jaw drops, stunned that it had been a random stranger.

Coach winks, "It does help to know where the action happens." He shrugs as if to feign modesty. He smacks Luke lightly on the bum, sending him off to the showers. As Luke walks away, he thinks, "Note to self: find more glory holes."

3

FIRST DAY

Puberty was kind to Luke—no longer the awkward teen. Still wiry but a bit more filled out. About 5'8", 130lbs. Blues eyes, dark blonde hair, a soft fuzz already covering his chest. Polos and khaki shorts fit his preppy look. He's also pretty sure he has a cute face because the girls really flirted with him senior year (not that he was interested).

Luke's parents drop him off at the dorm a week before school starts. Training begins the week before school. He's unpacking when his new roommate, Tom, walks in. They make their introductions. Tom is here on a full wrestling scholarship, a high school champ from the neighboring state. Luke thinks having a teammate will be helpful with the practice times required. They make small talk while they unpack. Luke is taking note of Tom's features. He's 5'10", 140-145, with lean muscle on his exposed legs and arms. Brown eyes, dark hair...on his arms and legs, too. As Tom bends over to pick up his next box to unpack, Luke's cock tingles at the sight of Tom's taught bubble butt in his gym shorts. Tom's style is more laid back than Luke is used to, t-shirt and elastic band shorts. Like he is on his way to or from the gym. "At least they are well fitting and not baggy," he thinks as he adjusts himself.

They've finished getting their room set, and Tom says he's sweaty and wants a shower before dinner. Tom pulls up his t-shirt revealing a dark furry chest and a nice treasure trail below his navel. Luke swallows, his mouth dry. Tom then shucks his gym shorts in one move to his ankles and steps out of them. He's wearing colorful briefs. They really show off his bubble butt. Tom grabs his towel, heads out the door to the showers, and says over his shoulder that he'll be back in a few. Luke looks down with relief that his khaki shorts did a good job of hiding his raging boner, but he can feel the wet spot spreading on his tighty whities.

Luke gets himself under control and heads to rinse himself before dinner. Wearing his shorts and taking fresh briefs with him, he passes Tom in the hall heading back to the room wearing only his towel. Luke wishes he'd stayed in the room a bit longer but remembers he has a whole semester for a peek.

The showers are stalls with shallow walls that provide little privacy. There are no curtains either. So you can see if a stall is taken because ass cheeks are always hanging out a little. There is also very little space to keep anything dry. Luke realizes Tom was smart to wear only his briefs to walk down the hall. Fortunately, since school doesn't start until next week, Luke has the shower to himself and can use several hooks to hang his things.

He steps into the farthest stall from the door. Luke isn't hard anymore but isn't completely soft, either. As Luke starts his shower, he debates if he should have a quick wank to prevent anything embarrassing from happening the rest of the evening. He's all lathered up in soap, and just about to give in to his urges, he hears the door shut. Whoever walked in is whistling what seems like random notes. Luke rinses the soap off as he hears the other person start their shower. He hears, "Hi. I'm Mike."

Luke slowly, awkwardly, leans back, looking around the wall. Mike is standing there in a bulging jockstrap, built like a refrigerator. 6'2", broad-shouldered, thick but not fat. The beard of a 20-year-old man, but a beard nonetheless. Hair everywhere, chest, belly, shoulders, even on his back. He sees as Mike turns to test the water temp.

"I'm Luke," he introduces himself.

Mike turns back, points to himself, "Football."

Luke says, "Makes sense," with a nod and a smirk.

"Let me guess... Track? Baseball?"

"Wrestling."

"Nice!" Mike says, nodding and chuckling. He puts his thumbs in the waistband of his jock and pulls them off in one fell swoop, sort of jump-roping out of them. Mike's large package jiggles. His balls aren't overly taught but definitely not saggy. They are large, his scrotum nearly the size of a softball. With only a quick glance before Luke turns back into his shower, he can tell Mike's cock is thick, and even though it's nicely perched on top of his ample balls, Luke can also tell it's a grower by the skin that covers most of his head. His shower now cold, Luke finishes up quickly before he gets hard and subsequently can't make it out of the bathroom. He says, "Nice to meet you," on his way past Mike's stall.

Tom is still in his briefs when Luke walks through the door. These are classic white like Luke's. He can tell by the outline that Tom is a bit of a show-er, with the ridge of his head more than halfway down his balls. There's also something about his scent. Not a smell, maybe like a pheromone that he learned about in science class. Something captivating. Between Mike's peep show and Tom in general, Luke can already feel another wet spot starting, so he dresses quickly. They go to the cafeteria together. Tom introduces him to a few other members of the wrestling team that are already there.

Some nice small talk makes Luke feel more settled in his new environment. Later Mike walks through and waves. Luke waves back.

Tom asks, "You know Mike?"

"We met in the shower."

One of the other boys shakes his head. "Hung like a beer can." They all chuckle.

Another guy gibes, "Jealous?"

The boy replies, "If I had one like that, I guess I'd show it off all the time, too." Several snicker at the joke. Luke enjoys how open and comfortable they seem. Talking about cock sizes and nudity. Luke is nervous about keeping his desires a secret but enthusiastic about the camaraderie and male bonding.

4

LATE NIGHT SHOWER

Luke's having trouble getting to sleep. First night in a new bed. Plus, his balls ache to be drained. Tom is asleep. Not snoring, but clearly out like a light. Luke pulls down his briefs and begins to stroke as quietly as he can, but the bed creaks when he makes too much movement. He's finally got a good slow rhythm going, and Tom switches sides. Luke freezes, waiting to make sure he hasn't woken up. Luke realizes this won't be productive, so he grabs his towel and heads to the showers.

To his surprise, he can hear a shower running as he gets near. As he enters the bathroom, he can tell by the broad shoulders and fuzzy back in the middle stall that it's Mike. He's not sure by the arm motion if Mike is lathering up or jerking off. Luke lets the door close, making its telltale noise. Mike leans back and looks as Luke nods hello. Mike looks a little sheepish, "Uh. I'm taking care of a little business...I hope that's ok."

Luke, in a rare moment of not being his normal, re-served self on such matters, says, "From the brief glimpse earlier, there's nothing little about it."

Mike makes a hearty laugh. As he laughs, he turns. Luke's eyes go wide involuntarily at the sight of Mike's cock. It's the size of a tall boy beer can. Mike holds it by the base and shakes it at Luke. "I like you, kid; you're funny." Luke laughs back, trying to recover from the sight. Mike asks, "You're cool if I finish, right?" as he turns back into his shower stall.

Luke swallows hard. Mike obviously has a ton of self-confidence. This empowers Luke a little, and he decides to be candid. "I'm...kind of here for the same reason." Mike says from behind the wall, "Cool, man. We all do it. I don't get why some guys are so embarrassed. Better out than in, I say."

Luke feels bolder now. He takes the stall next to Mike. He begins to stroke. Luke has a very average cut cock, but veiny and hard as steel. His eyes are closed. He plays with his nipples, then tugs his balls while stroking. He can hear the fapping noises Mike is making. This makes it hotter. Luke's got a good rhythm going, lost in the sensation. He doesn't notice the change in the sound of water hitting the floor in Mike's stall. He jumps as Mike says from right behind him, "Let's see what you're working with, buddy?"

Luke freezes. Does Mike know he's into guys? Is this a trick? Or hazing? Luke turns slightly, looking like a deer in headlights. Mike says, "Oh. Sorry, buddy. Didn't mean to freak you out. Have you never circle-jerked with your buds before?" Luke shook his head no, still wide-eyed." Mike, "My bad. Sorry. (awkward pause) Is that something you'd be cool with?" Luke swallows, "I...guess." "Cool," Mike smiles," Just buds having a good time."

Luke finishes turning towards Mike, cock standing straight out. Mike looks down, "Nice one, man. That's a good size." Luke half smiles at the compliment. Mike shakes his hard cock once, "Guys think it's great to have a big dick, but really it can be hard finding a girl willing to try. And forget about a blow job." Mike reaches out and squeezes Luke's cock. Luke tries not to jump at his touch. "Wow." Mike says, "That is rock hard. You could hammer a nail through a board with that thing. I'm at full mast, and mine's still kind of spongy, see." Mike thrusts forward, offering Luke a feel, still holding Luke's cock. Another awkward moment passes as neither moves.

Then slowly, Luke reaches out and squeezes. It's the first penis that wasn't his he's touched. He notices the sheer girth of it. The heft and weight. But then, yes... spongy. It's erect, firm even, but nothing like Luke's own. Mike strokes Luke. "Yeah, that's nice and hard. You could get into the tightest of holes with that thing." Luke slowly strokes Mike, noticing the skin sliding with his hand, not under. Back and forth. Longer strokes, now feeling the full length.

Mike says, "Yeah. That feels great. Would you be OK jerking each other off?"

Luke is speechless but nods. Mike closes his eyes, and each finds a nice rhythm to stroke the other.

After a few minutes, Luke is lost in bliss when Mike says, "I'm getting close. Would you finish me, then I'll finish you?" Luke doesn't really know what he means but says, "Sure."

Mike turns around, taking Luke's arm to show him how to reach around him. Luke sees how this is more comfortable, like jerking his own cock. He strokes faster as Mike breathes harder. Mike's really working his nipples. Luke's cock is pointing upward, wedged in Mike's crack. Mike is thrusting his hips, rubbing Luke's cock against him in the process. Luke is in heaven. The rubbing makes Luke jerk faster. Luke's hips and cock thrust on autopilot as Mike thrusts into his jerking fist. Mike says he's going to cum. Luke squeezes a little more while jerking faster. He can feel the huge pulses through Mike's cock. His spunk splatters the wall across from them—one spurt after another. Luke can't believe someone can produce so much spunk. He slows his motions as the volleys come to an end; he lets go and gently backs away from Mike.

Mike finally recovers and turns around. "Damn, buddy. That was incredible."

Luke smiles with pride. "Not a bad first time jerking off someone else," he thinks to himself.

Mike's still semi-hard, oozing the last of his load. "Now it's your turn," Mike says with a devilish grin. He motions for Luke to turn and face the shower. Mike wraps his big arms around Luke. One hand on his cock, the other tugging his balls. He begins to stroke. Luke can feel Mike's fat cock running down his crack, like a fat hotdog on top of a too-tiny bun. Mike's stroke is excellent, just grazing Luke's tightly cut cock.

Mike whispers in his ear, "That's a great cock, buddy. So firm. Great for stroking." His words drive Luke closer to the edge. He can feel Mike's cock start to get hard again, rising into his crack. He can feel his nuts begin to draw up as he gets closer. Mike tightens his finger and thumb around Luke's sack and tugs gently, keeping his nuts from tightening. The sensation is incredible. Mike seems to be an expert and jerking. Luke hopes to learn more from him but, for now, gets lost in the sensations.

Mike is harder still, knowing he's getting Luke close. Mike's fat cock head grazes Luke's hole. That's all it takes. Luke's whole body spasms. Mike says in his ear, " Yeah, buddy. Shoot that spunk for me. Drain those balls." As Luke begins to cum, Mike lets go of his balls, letting them draw up and shoot all they contain. Luke nearly collapses as his orgasm subsides.

Mike says, "Man, that load was almost as big as mine." Luke smiles. Mike goes back to his shower to rinse and finish up. They say their good nights and return to their rooms. Luke falls asleep almost instantly.

5

FIRST PRACTICE

Early morning the next day for workout and first practice. A majority of the team are new freshmen; he met most of them at dinner last night. They divide up based on weight class. Luke manages to "shake the rust off" pretty quickly, just like when he was younger. He realizes he really is a natural at the sport. Even though he hasn't actively wrestled in years, he manages to keep up with, if not best, his teammates. Luke also likes the way his singlet feels. Like an old blanket. But he's also glad he got drained so thoroughly last night because the way it rubs him also feels a little sensual.

Coach gives pointers and tips during various matches. Luke is making mental notes about his teammates' moves. His new roomie, Tom, is also quite good. He hasn't been pinned yet. Coach has been pairing some matches where someone in a lower class is up against someone with a weight advantage. Tom has a stalemate in one of these matches. Luke is impressed.

It's getting close to time to break for lunch, and Coach says, "Last match...calling Tom and Luke to the mat."

Tom has the advantage on nearly every front, but

Luke manages to keep him at bay. Even though he's in the moment, concentrating on winning, he still manages to notice when their cocks touch, rubbing together as they struggle. Or when a hand near the balls pulls a thigh to pin the opponent. Luke is starting to tire. Tom's got him in a difficult hold. Luke, on instinct, remembers a move he used to pull when he was younger, twisting himself free and using Tom's own weight against him to get him off balance. Luke's got him pinned; now, to just hold him for the count. Tom's scent. It's stronger now. Luke ignores it, stays in the moment. Coach calls it for Luke. Everyone cheers.

Tom looks a little miffed as he gets up but gives Luke a hand to get up from the mat. Luke thinks he may have insulted Tom because he won't look him in the face. But then he realizes that Tom is looking at his crotch. Luke looks down. Not only is he raging hard, but has a big wet spot to boot. Tom just says, "Good match." as he walks toward the showers. Luke is mortified. He trudges dejectedly towards the shower room. Not only couldn't he control it, but he didn't even notice it was happening. What will he do during a match? "At least everyone else was walking toward the showers; I don't think they saw," he thinks, "Will Tom tell everyone?" As Luke looks up, he realizes someone else did see. Coach.

"You want to talk, kid?"

Luke shrugs an affirmative, and he changes course into Coach's office.

"Your worst fear, huh?" Coach says. Luke just nods, not looking up to avoid eye contact. "Look, son. It happens to all of us. Myself included. You can't control it all the time. It's a natural response for a lot of guys. You'll see. It'll happen to others on the team. You won't be the only one. We all just ignore it and walk it off." Coach puts a gentle hand on Luke's shoulder. He'd forgotten how Coach can make everything feel ok.

The weight of embarrassment lightens. Luke looks up and says, "Thanks, Coach."

"Anytime sport. Now go shower; you stink." They both laugh.

up and says, "Thanks, Coach."

※ 6 ※

TOM AND LUKE

Luke wants to try to catch Tom alone, partially because of besting him on the mat but also to somehow play down the erection he got. But there are too many people around during lunch. And Luke has to rush across campus for a meeting about his work-study job.

Because of his class and practice schedule and his familiarity with the gym facilities from being on an athletic team, they offer him an evening job at the campus gym. Like most community colleges, this one is in a smaller town. The school lets local alumni have a membership in the evenings to help offset the cost, and students can also get access. His duties include resetting weight equipment when people don't put it back, laundry, restocking towels, and sweeping and mopping the locker rooms. Basic stuff. His orientation takes way longer than expected, and he has just enough time for a quick dinner before starting his first shift that evening.

Just as his job was described, he checks people in at the desk and returns dumbbells and barbells to the racks because of the inconsiderate lifters.

He folds and restocks towels. Each locker room has a sauna and steam room, so they go through plenty. He gets quite an eye full in the locker with some older locals. Who knew balls could be that saggy? He glimpses his first uncut cock while the guys towel off in the shower. He wasn't sure, but he could have sworn two middle-aged guys were up to something in the steam room, but the glass door was too foggy to be sure.

Fortunately, the gym closes at 8:00 pm. Plus, he only had to work a few days each week. The locker room views might end up being a bonus he hadn't expected.

As Luke enters the room, Tom is on the bed in a different-colored pair of briefs. "Where have you been?"

"I started work study today."

"Cool."

Luke shoe-gazes, "About today..."

Tom says, "That was some move." Luke looks up. Tom is smiling ear to ear. Luke's tension eases. "You're gonna have to teach me how to get out of a hold like that." Tom gets off the bed walking toward him, hand up for a high-five. Luke responds in kind, smiling. As the high-five passes, Tom goes in for a hug. Luke isn't prepared but quickly responds by hugging back. He can feel Tom's cock right next to his; Luke is rapidly hardening.

Tom says, "Glad you're on our team," and squeezes a little before ending the hug.

Luke's pants are tenting. Luke looks down, red with embarrassment again. Luke looks up to see Tom looking at his tent pole.

"Don't worry about that either," Tom says, "happens to me all the time."

Luke now notices that Tom's cock is rising but constrained in his briefs. Tom steps closer and says softly, "I didn't just mean on the wrestling team." Tom gently wraps his hand around the back of Luke's head, pulling him in for a kiss. Luke's mouth moves on instinct to accept. His first kiss. Perfection. Some tongue, not too much. Not too wet or dry. It feels in slow motion and forever.

Luke's arms are by his side, not that he notices. Tom grabs one and pulls it around his back. Luke follows with the other. Tom moves the one he's holding down toward his ass. Luke squeezes his taught bubble butt while thrusting his tongue deeper into Tom's mouth. The kiss becomes more frantic, passionate. Tom lifts Luke's shirt over his head. Luke removes his shorts. They kiss again, their brief-covered cocks rubbing against each other. Luke reaches down to point his upward to be more comfortable, the head just peering above the waistband.

Tom looks down to see. He uses his thumb to wipe a large drool of pre-cum from Luke's cock, then licks it from his finger. Luke swallows hard, his mouth suddenly dry. Tom adjusts himself the same way while Luke watches. But Tom shows an inch of shaft plus the head above the waistband. Luke rubs Tom's chest hair as they kiss, Tom guiding them to the bed.

They hump and frottage, lying on the bed. Luke doesn't want the kissing to end. Tom has other plans. He nibbles his way down Luke's neck to his nipple and lightly bites. Luke gasps in pleasure. Not only from the nipple play but Tom's treasure trail against his exposed cock head. Tom works his way down, removing Luke's briefs. In one slow movement, Tom engulfs Luke's cock in his warm mouth, all the way nose to bush. Luke's eyes roll back in his head. He never imagined it would feel this incredible.

Tom works his tongue like a whirlwind while slowly bobbing. He reaches up and gently twists both nips. Luke wants it to last, but he can't hold out. He begins to cum. Tom swallows every spurt. Luke loses count of how many shots he makes, but it's more than he's ever done before. Tom keeps Luke's cock in his mouth until every last drop has oozed out. Tom crawls up and kisses him. Luke has tasted his own cum before, but it tastes even better in Tom's mouth as they kiss. Luke likes the kissing but wants to taste his first cock more. He's not subtle. He flips Tom off of him onto his back and quickly strips him of his briefs.

Tom's cock is a beauty. Luke's is around 6 inches. Tom's has to be 7 inches or a little more. It's slightly slimmer than Luke's but not thin by any means. He's got a thick bush too. There's a nice little dribble of pre-cum. Luke uses his tongue to lap it up. He loves the taste and the slickness of it. He repeats what Tom did, slowly working his way down. The sensation is incredible. Luke is instantly hard again with Tom in his mouth. He tries to go all the way to the bottom like Tom did but starts to gag. Tom gently tells him, "You don't have to take it all." Luke nods, most of it still in his mouth. He slowly moves up and down the shaft. Tom whispers, "Swirl your tongue." Luke complies. Tom moans loudly, his cock flexing in Luke's mouth. Luke can taste another drop of precum.

He understands now. More tongue, less bobbing. He works his tongue in a circle just under the head. Tom moans, "Yes, that's the spot." Luke varies the motions of his tongue, testing what makes Tom's cock flex. Tom says, "You're a natural," as he runs his fingers through Luke's hair. Tom starts to thrust his cock in and out of Luke's mouth. Slow, shallow thrusts. Luke reaches up to play with Tom's nipples. He gives them a tweak, and Tom thrusts deeper while moaning, "Harder, baby." Luke pinches them. Tom thrusts faster. "Yeah, baby. Work my nips." Luke works his tongue as fast as he can while twisting and pulling Tom's nips.

Tom's hips buck wildly. "Fuck. Yeah. Here it comes." Tom's load unleashes in Luke's mouth. Luke swallows the first volley, but the second and third come too quickly. It's more than he can swallow; it oozes out around the shaft. Tom holds his head, thrusting.

Luke does his best not to gag. "At least he isn't thrusting too deep," he thinks. Tom slows and lets go of

Luke's head. Luke pulls off Tom's cock and swallows, then laps up what's on his shaft and head. He realizes he loves the taste. Much better than his own. Tom pulls Luke up on top of him to kiss him deeply. Then he licks some of his own cum on Luke's chin to help clean him up.

"That was your first time, wasn't it?" Tom asks.

"Was it that bad?"

"Quite the opposite. You did really well for a first time. But I'll work on teaching you how to swallow big loads," Tom winks.

Luke smiles at him, and they kiss some more. They drift off to sleep in each other's arms.

❧ 7 ❧

TOWEL BOY

Luke is working his fourth shift for the week in the gym. He's been working every evening with Melissa, another student. She's been working at the gym since last fall semester. She tells him, "Enjoy this slow week; it can get busy once students are back."

She helps Luke learn all the "shortcuts" to make the job easier to handle. He's gotten the routine down pretty well for the week. Folding towels fresh from the laundry seems never-ending. They take turns manning the front desk every fifteen minutes to walk the floor, ensure weights are put back correctly, and that machines look cleaned off. Every hour they each go check their respective locker room. Pick up towels. Wipe down sinks. Replace empty TP rolls. Check that the sauna and steam room are functioning and for lost items or left towels. Luke notices some guests are quite sloppy, leaving towels on the floor, even in the steam room. Someone has left a bottle of liniment in the steam room, which now smells of menthol and eucalyptus. He collects the occasional pair of swim trunks left behind on a hook after the person showered.

It's Luke's last walk-through of the night, just before closing. No one is in the locker room, so he sweeps near the lockers, mops quickly near the steam room and showers, picks up towels, and gathers the trash. As he returns from dropping the used towels in the laundry room, he notices a pair of skimpy red Speedos on a hook. He guessed he'd been looking at the floor for towels and didn't notice it before. He finishes his routine in the shower area by stretching out each stall's curtain to dry out.

As he finishes, he hears a noise in the steam room. As he opened the door, a blast of steam hit him in the face making it hard to see, but he could see enough. A man stood in the middle, his back to the door. He was middle-aged, fit, with dark hair and a Speedo tan line. As the steam cleared slightly, He realized there was another man in front of that man...bent over bracing on the bench in the steam room, swim trunks around his ankles. From what little he could see around the first man, the second was fair-skinned, a bit thicker build, and enjoying getting pounded in the ass. Although it felt like minutes in slow motion as Luke's eyes absorbed as much as they could, it was mere seconds. Luke's knee-jerk reaction was to awkwardly say, "Uhhhh, ten minutes 'til closing," while shutting the door and walking out of the locker room red-faced. Fortunately, Melissa was across the gym wiping down machines before she went to do the women's locker room, so he didn't have to explain his flush cheeks.

A few minutes later, the fair-skinned man left the locker room. Even though he'd obviously showered quickly, he was still red-faced and sweaty from the steam room exposure. Luke thought, "And maybe from getting off as well." He was stockier than Luke could tell earlier, maybe 40ish, with sandy brown hair. He had a cute, round, clean-shaven face that made him look younger, and kind eyes. Because he failed to button his shirt all the way up in haste, the gap exposes the soft, brown fur covering the man's chest. The man sheepishly nods hello at Luke as he hands over the locker key to get his car keys back. Luke smiles and gently nods back with a half wink, hoping the man understands, "Your secret is safe." Luke can see the man's shoulder relax a bit as he turns toward the exit. Luke watches the man exit, thinking how he can't wait to tell Tom.

He jumps as someone says, "Evening, Luke." Luke hadn't realized that the other man had exited the locker room. He also didn't know the other man was Coach.

"Evening, Coach," Luke says as he takes his locker key to the peg board. "Have a good workout?"

"Best I've had in a long time." Coach pauses. "I don't get the opportunity to exercise how I'd like."

Luke understands. "I can imagine that with a schedule like yours, it would be difficult to find time to fit in. And I'm sure there are limitations to the kinds of exercise you can do around here."

Coach smiles. His face is the same understanding face that had made Luke comfortable so many times before, but this time it shows that he appreciates being understood.

"See you at practice tomorrow. Get some rest," Coach says as he exits the gym.

❧ 8 ❧

BEARS

"You'll never believe what happened at the gym tonight," Luke says, bursting into the dorm room. Tom is naked on his bed, reading a comic. Luke just stares at his beautiful cock. Eventually, Tom asks, "And? What happened." Luke snaps out of it and repeats the story.

"And then I turn around, and it was Coach!" Luke is incredulous.

Tom just laughs. "My gaydar always pinged a little with Coach, but sounds like he might be into bears."

"Bears?" Luke asks.

"Bigger guys, body hair, beards. You know."

Luke ponders. That makes Mike a bear. He did think the man was cute, also. "Hmm, that's something to explore," he thinks to himself.

"I only saw a few seconds, but Coach was really pounding him good. If I'd known it was Coach, I would have tried to get a better look."

Tom just winks as he laughs and leans in for a kiss. Tom is hard from hearing the story; his precum dribbles on the back of Luke's hand as they kiss. Luke was already rock hard, but now it's pulsing on its own against his shorts. He pulls away to undress.

"Have you ever done butt stuff?" Luke asks.

"Sure." Tom replies, "Fingering, prostate massage, top, bottom."

Luke, now naked, stands there looking a bit bewildered. He figured Tom would be more experienced than himself. He's guessing he may have underestimated. After a pause, he asks, "Will you teach me?"

"Sure. Where do you want to start?"

Luke thinks for a minute. "Fingering sounds like a good start. What's prostate massage?"

"Oh ho ho," Tom comically evil laughs, "you'll see."

Tom drags his mattress to the floor between their beds since the frames in the dorm squeak so much. He lays down a towel and gets some lube from his drawer. He has Luke lie on his stomach. "Now it's important to relax. Just take a deep breath in, then relax on the exhale. If something hurts, say so." Tom squirts lube on his fingers and rubs some on Luke's hole. Luke breathes in sharply at the wonderful sensation. Tom gently rubs his hole and applies a little bit of pressure. "Breathe in and hold." Luke does as he's told. "Now relax as you exhale." As Luke breathes out, his whole body, including his hole, relaxes a little. The bit of pressure Tom is applying lets his finger slip right into the second knuckle. Luke sighs at the pleasurable sensation. Tom dribbles a little more lube on Luke's crack, letting it run down to his finger. Tom works this lube into Luke's hole to make sure he has enough in there. Luke squirms in pleasure as the finger goes in and out. "Another breath," Tom says.

As Luke exhales, Tom's finger goes all the way in. Luke moans loudly. He feels Tom wiggle his finger a bit, and then a wave of euphoria rushes over him. Tom expertly applies pressure to Luke's prostate.

Luke involuntarily makes an "Ohhhh," rising in pitch as it draws on with each pulse Tom makes with his finger. "That, my boy, is prostate massage." Luke only barely hears him, his eyes rolling back into his head. Tom slides his finger in and out a few times, switching from the forefinger to the middle to get deeper. With his middle finger all the way in, he applies some pressure to Luke's hole: North, South, East, West. Loosening it. Stretching it. Tom pulls his finger out and stacks the middle finger on top of the forefinger. He gets the two tips in easily.

"Breathe again. Relax," he tells Luke. This time, as Luke exhales, Tom gets both fingers in up to the second knuckle. Luke makes a lower "Oh" sound.

"You good?" Tom asks.

"Oh, yeah," Luke replies.

Tom gently rotates from horizontal to vertical. Luke moans loudly. "Let's try something different."

Tom gets Luke on all fours, covers his cock with plenty of lube, and lines it up with Luke's hole. He applies just enough pressure to hold his cock's aim. Even after the two fingers, Luke's hole is still tight. "Now, as you breathe out this time, you push back into me at your own pace. You're in control," Tom says.

Luke breathes in, then out, but doesn't move. One more breath in. "Relax," he thinks. He loosens his shoulders and exhales, letting go of tension in the rest of his body. He pushes back, there's a little pressure, but he focuses on relaxing. And just like that, Tom's cock head gently slides past his tight little pucker. Luke gasps in ecstasy as he backs all the way, feeling Tom's bush on his ass checks. It's not completely comfortable, but the pleasure outweighs the pain.

"Congrats, Luke. You just lost your cherry." Tom spanks him playfully on the ass cheek. Luke moves forward and backward a few times slowly. He gets why so many men love it, but his freshly deflowered hole can't really take the friction of thrusting yet.

He tells Tom, "I understand."

"I wanted your first test run to be gentle," Tom says, gently pulling out. "Now it's my turn." He plops down on the mattress next to Luke.

Luke follows the same steps of loosening Tom's hole. He finds his prostate. Tom gives him instructions on how to apply pressure for pleasure. Luke notices Tom is good at relaxing, and it's easy for him to slip in two fingers.

Tom says, "I'm ready," as he rolls over onto his back. Luke looks a little confused as Tom pulls his legs up into the air. Tom smirks, "I want to see your face when you cum in me. It's your first fuck, after all."

Luke grabs Tom's ankles. Tom helps line up Luke's cock head to his hole. "When I breathe out, slowly push in," Tom says. Luke tries to be gentle. Tom relaxes with his breath, and Luke slides right in. It's so tight and so warm. He's all the way in but not sure what to do. Tom looks him in the eyes. "Fuck me."

Luke begins to thrust. Tom starts jerking his cock. Tom moans, giving Luke the confidence he needs. He takes longer thrusts. "Yeah. Fuck me harder." Luke thrusts harder. Tom moans louder with each thrust. The lust takes over Luke. He begins to thrust like a wild man, an animal. He grunts with every thrust. His balls tighten.

He whispers, "I'm gonna cum. I'm gonna cum. I'm gonna cum."

Tom moans. "Shoot it in me. Fill me with your spunk."

Luke takes a powerful thrust, the full length of his shaft, and then stops, buried deep in Tom. He feels Tom's hole squeeze and pulse against his shaft. Tom is cumming spurt after spurt on his chest as Luke cums deep in his ass. After the first few volleys, Luke begins to thrust again, trying to extend his orgasm. Tom moans, "Yes. Yes. Harder." Luke obeys. Tom has another orgasm, this time covering his face and the wall behind him.

Luke's own orgasm subsides, and he pulls out and falls on the mattress next to Tom. After they catch their breath, Tom says, "Next time, I'm gonna fill up your tight hole."

Luke replies, "I look forward to it."

They clean up the room and head to the shower to clean up before sleep.

9

FIRST MATCH

Over the next couple of weeks, they suck each other off almost every night. As promised, Tom has filled Luke's hole with a substantial load a few times. The last time, Luke was on his back and managed to cum hands-free. Even Tom was impressed. Tom, of course, has returned the favor, letting Luke try doggie style, or cowboy style, with Tom riding him, just to give him the full experience.

Today is their first wrestling match. Luke is feeling good about it. Practice has been going well. He's competing as if he hadn't given it up for a few years. His match starts; they are both pretty evenly matched. He quickly gets his opponent in a hold from behind. The other guy manages to make his way out of it and get Luke into a hold. Luke gets out without much effort and flips into a hold where they are each facing outward. The boys squirm around to face each other, struggling to gain dominance in the match. Suddenly Luke feels a familiar feeling. A hard cock against his belly...his opponent's.

"Coach was right," he thinks. He's distracted, and the guy breaks free and pins Luke from behind. Luke can feel the erection rubbing between his ass cheeks. Luke can feel his own cock beginning to plump. The fear gives him a power boost. He breaks free. He gets the other guy pinned, but their cocks rub against each other as they struggle. The ref begins the count. Luke wins. They break apart.

The other guy offers a handshake. "Good match," he says. Luke is baffled. It's like he doesn't even know his boner is showing. He could care less.

It's all Luke can think about. He manages to say, "Thank you," as they shake hands. Luke hunches over in a failed attempt to hide his erection. Adding to his horror, he notices he has a huge wet spot visible. He sits watching the rest of his teammates' matches, trying not to make contact with anyone.

Coach comes up to him in the locker room. Most of the other guys are in the showers. "Great match today, champ."

"Thanks," he says in a down tone.

Coach puts a calming hand on Luke's shoulder. "You did notice the other guy, right? I told you it happens to everyone."

Luke looks around. Then softly, "But I had a giant wet spot, too!"

Coach laughs. "So? You're a leaker. You'll be grateful for that in other situations." Luke just shrugs.

Coach has his stern voice on now. "That guy didn't notice. And he was up close. I didn't see anyone pointing or staring. Everyone that likes this sport knows that it's natural, and it happens whether the person wants it to or not. I saw it when it caught you by surprise. But you managed to keep your head in the game and win—this time. Ignore your embarrassment. You're an athlete. Focus on the sport. Plus, that was a great match. Even that guy knew it. He acknowledged it with that handshake."

Luke knows Coach is right. But he still wishes he'd had better control.

Coach softens his voice now. "Remember how I... exercise?"

Luke looks up at him, puzzled as to where this is going.

"I'm sure you exercise daily." Pausing as he finds the words. "Even if you don't have a spotter, you probably exercise by yourself."

Luke nods, understanding the metaphor.

"Maybe you should exercise right before a match." Coach shrugs. "Just a thought."

Luke thinks Coach might be onto something.

The Gym has settled into a regular rhythm now that school is a few weeks into the semester. The initial rush of students has waned to just the regulars, and they usually finish by 6:00 or 6:30 so they can hit the cafeteria before closing. Luke also notices that few, if any, of the students use the locker rooms. They come in workout clothes and shower in the dorms. A few football players may come through and use the steam room after practice, but that's it.

During practice earlier that day, Luke landed hard on his shoulder. Coach had come in early to use some of the cardio machines. He asked Luke about his shoulder, and Luke said it was OK, but that was at the beginning of his shift. Now it is quite tender to move, making towel folding a slower task than usual.

Coach comes out of the locker room and notices Luke is struggling with the towels. "Are you sure about that shoulder, bud?"

Luke says, "It does hurt more than before." Coach walks into the gym office and returns with some over-the-counter pain relievers, anti-inflammatory pills. Nancy, the evening manager, follows Coach out.

She says, "Coach says you had a bad tumble earlier today."

Luke replies, "I just landed hard on the mat." He

swallows the pills with water from the dispenser beside the front desk.

Coach says, "You might want to try the sauna. Help loosen those muscles. Then get a good night's sleep."

Nancy nods in agreement. "There's only an hour left before we close, Luke. Go ahead. There's only a few regulars left. We can finish towels tomorrow."

Luke says he appreciates it, grabs a locker key for his clothes, and says goodnight to Coach as they depart in different directions.

The sauna is a nice size and has an L-shaped bench with two levels. He doesn't bother turning on the light; plenty is coming through the glass door from the locker room. Since no one else is there, Luke lays out naked on a towel on one of the upper benches. He tries to relax his whole body. After a few minutes, he realizes Coach was right, and his shoulder doesn't hurt as bad as it did. He enjoys the dry heat. Getting comfortable, he's just about to doze off when the door opens. Luke looks up, not at the man, but to make sure he's not blocking all the bench space. Then he turns to the person walking in. The man is backlit, so he's unsure who it is, but Luke asks, "Do you want me to get up?" "No," the man replies in a kind voice, " there's plenty of room for me on the other bench."

Luke closes his eyes again as he lays back down. He can hear the man climb up and sit on the other upper bench. "I'm Rob, by the way."

"I'm Luke," he says before looking up and then realizing he recognizes the man. It's Coach's "friend" from a few weeks ago. Luke has seen him work out a few times since then and has always been polite, but noticed that his locker room time has been brief. The way the light is coming through the door, Luke can get a better look than he's been able to before. He's wearing his towel, but his legs are stocky and fuzzy, not overly hairy, but he thinks it makes them look manly.

His chest and belly have soft brown short fur all over. He has a bit of a belly, not too big, and his chest is flabby. Luke finds it odd; he wants to hug the man. There's something teddy bearish about him. That also makes him attractive to Luke. Trying to defuse his awkwardness, Luke says, "Oh hi, yes, I've seen you in before. I must have missed you coming in to work out earlier."

Rob smiles, his cheeks a bit red, "I just got here to use the sauna. Rough day at work." Luke nods in understanding, then lays back down. He rotates his shoulder and arm in a bunch of directions. "Did you hurt something?" the man asks.

"Landed wrong in practice," Luke replies.

"Oh. Sorry to hear that. I do massage on the side. Would you like me to work on it a little?"

Luke sits up. "That would be great. Sure you don't mind?"

"Not at all."

Luke wraps his towel around his waist, "Nice to officially meet."

They shake hands, and Luke sits between Rob's legs on the lower bench. Rob goes to work.

Luke realizes how much it still hurts. To distract himself from the initial pain, he asks, "Massage on the side?"

Rob answers while he works, "Yes. I'm an accountant to pay the bills. I took a class in Massage back in college. Here, in fact. I really enjoyed the therapy aspect of it, but there's also a bit of Zen for me. I can zone out on the stress and baggage of my day job. I have a little studio in my home, but I don't have any regular clients. I have listings on a few sites, so I get to do it occasionally."

As Rob moves Luke's arm in different directions and applies pressure with his other hand, Luke notices the pain is already much better. "The heat in here is making the work go faster," Rob says as if he knew what Luke was thinking.

Rob works Luke's neck, shoulders, and upper back. Luke's never had a massage before, but he definitely wants to again. Luke's head is leaning forward while Rob works. Luke opens his eyes to see his full erection standing up between the ends of the towel. He tries to cover it.

Rob says, "That happens to most guys when they get this relaxed. Nothing to be ashamed of."

"Coach says the same thing," Luke mumbles.

"Coach is a smart guy. One of the best people I know."

Luke doesn't know what comes over him, but before he even realizes it, he asks, "Do you two know each other well?"

"Well, it IS a small town, so everyone knows everyone, but I'd say we're friends. We do get to spend some time together on occasion, but not often."

Luke swallows. "Do you have many friends here?"

Rob sighs, "Not really. The odd acquaintance or a friend who travels through once in a while."

Luke feels possessed like he can't control what he's saying. "Would you like me to be your friend?"

He can hear the smile in Rob's voice, "That is awfully kind of you, but most of my friends are usually a bit older than me."

"Oh," Luke sounds dejected, "that makes sense."

"Do you not have ANY friends of your own?" Rob asks.

"I do. But it's fairly new," Luke pauses, "I guess I'm just curious about different types of friends and the things they might do together. You know, how different people have different hobbies." Luke thinks to himself that he's getting really good at talking in code.

After a pause, Rob says thoughtfully, "Maybe you're just looking for a mentor."

Luke turns to look up at Rob. "Maybe you're right."

Rob says, "Speak plainly. Not doublespeak."

Luke stands up to face Rob and looks him in the eyes. His cock is sticking straight out from the towel still. Luke has never been so candid, "There's something about you. I can't decide if I want you to bear hug me or let me do what Coach did."

Rob's eyes widen, "Well. That is quite bold, young man," as he gets up, stepping down to floor level with Luke. Luke has to back up a little to give him room. Rob grabs Luke's cock with one hand and the back of his head with the other while going in for a kiss. Luke meets him halfway, their tongues swirling around each other. Luke's hands instinctively go to Rob's chest, rubbing his fur and working his nips. He can't believe how rubbing Rob's belly makes his cock flex. Rob pulls back, "You're in charge. Tell Daddy what you want, son."

Luke leans in, then softly but firmly says, "Bend over." Rob turns around and takes his towel off. Luke sees he has light fuzz on his back but thick fur on his ass cheeks. Rob folds the towel on the upper bench and leans on it with his elbows. Luke realizes he doesn't have any lube.

Rob can sense his hesitation, "Spit on it." Luke freezes. Rob more gently, "Spit a good loogie on my hole and the tip of your cock. Don't worry. Daddy can take it. I'm gonna mentor you in the old ways."

Luke spreads Rob's hairy cheeks and hocks a good one just above his pucker, letting it dribble down. Then another on his cock head. He lines up his cock to Rob's hole, and before he can do anything else, Rob slides all the way back. "Now pump me full of jizz, boy. I need a good fucking after the day I've had." Luke does as he says. He begins to thrust. Rob's hairy ass is driving him crazy. He's pulling out for full strokes and pushing in as hard as he can. Rob groans with each thrust. Luke's thrusts get shorter and faster as he gets closer to cumming.

"Yeah, boy. Fill my hole," Rob says as he starts to jerk his own cock, "That's it, boy. You're gonna make me cum with that hard cock." That sends Luke over the edge. One deep thrust and all his spunk fills Rob's hole. Luke can feel it oozing out around his cock and into his pubes. He's never felt a load that big before.

Rob is still jerking fast as a madman, "Leave it in, boy. Daddy's close." Luke reaches around and takes Rob's dick in his hand. It's barely 5 inches long, but there's a gap between his finger and thumb. By comparison, it makes Mike's dick feel normal-sized. It's like jerking a soup can. Rob grabs his nips, and Luke starts to thrust with his still-hard cock.

"Fuck yeah, son. Fuck the cum outta me." Luke jerks and fucks faster. Suddenly, Rob's hole clenches down on his cock. He can feel his prostate throb against his cock as the bench is doused in Rob's cum. They catch their breath. Rob uses his towel to clean the bench. Rob says, "I guess I should mentor some." He winks as Luke chuckles. "Spit is ok for those with enough experience. I get tested regularly, but you shouldn't be fucking strangers without condoms. You're a considerate lover. But sometimes, bottoms just want to get fucked. Other times, they want to get fucked to cum. And variations in between. Be clear with your communication. It can be better for everyone. Have a good one, kid."

"Thanks, Rob. I appreciate the insight...and everything else." Luke winks.

Luke gets back to the dorm room. Before Tom can say hello, Luke says, "I think I have a thing for bears..."

Tom's cock is already starting to harden, "Do tell. Exciting night at the gym?" Tom reaches for the lube, so he can stroke and enjoy the story he's about to hear.

*

10

MORE THE MERRIER

Campus is pretty empty on Saturdays. Most students go home for the weekend. Tom has a car, so he and Luke decide to goof off in the next town over at their annual festival on the square. It's a nice day of fair food, kooky arts and crafts, mediocre rides, and some surprisingly decent live music. The boys finish the day with a movie at the cinema, which they had to themselves because of the festival.

It's late when they get back to the dorm. All is quiet since it's mostly empty. On the way to their room, they can hear the water running in the dorm showers. Luke takes a quick peek, and sure enough, it's Mike. He gently closes the door. "I think Mike's about to have some alone time," Luke says with a devilish grin. "Should we join him?"

Tom doesn't answer; he just takes off, racing to their room. Luke catches up. Once inside, they both strip, slinging clothes everywhere, wrap their towels around their naked waists, and run back to the shower. Luke gently closes the door behind them. They quietly hang their towels on the hooks and then make their way over toward Mike. Mike is facing into the stall, his arm working a mile a minute.

"Having a good time?" Luke says.

Mike jumps as they caught him off guard. He turns, a bit in shock. Once he realizes it's Luke, he laughs. "Hey, buddy. Yeah, I'm enjoying it." Tom's jaw drops. He's seen Mike in the showers before, but never at full mast. "Tom, right?" Mike sticks out his hand for a shake. Tom shakes his hand, never breaking eye contact with his crotch.

Mike laughs, "This one is funny. Ya'll here for the same reason, I guess?"

Luke says, "You've guessed correctly," and laughs. Luke and Tom each turn on a shower on either side of Mike, rinse a bit, and turn to face each other, making three sides of a square to watch each other jerk. Luke is pretty sure Mike is turned on by Tom's attention to his big cock.

Mike stops wanking, looks at Tom, and motions to his cock. He says, "You want to give it a go?" Tom nods as he reaches out and begins to stroke Mike. Mike reaches over and takes Tom's cock in return. "That's a nice one, Tom. About as long as mine." Tom looks up for the first time and smiles at him. Mike takes his other hand, moving Luke's hand out of the way to stroke Luke also.

"It's like skiing," Mike says. They all laugh. After a bit, Mike looks at Luke, "You wanna give it a go again?"

Luke says, "I sure do." Luke and Tom swap hands on Mike's cock. Luke moves in front of him for a different angle. He kneels, and before Mike can say anything, Luke manages to get the head and several inches in his mouth.

"Whoa...Oh....OOOHHHH," Mike moans. It feels even thicker in Luke's mouth. He's proud he's managed to get this much in. He's really working his tongue around like Tom taught him. Mike gently rests his free hand on top of Luke's head. He closes his eyes and leans his head back. Tom reaches over to work his nipples while Mike continues to stroke him.

Mike finally says, "This is my first real blow job. It feels incredible." Luke works on Mike's cock a while longer, Mike moaning low the whole time.

Tom taps Luke on the shoulder, "My turn." They swap. Mike strokes Luke's cock now while Luke runs his fingers through Mike's furry chest. Luke's cock is so hard it almost hurts. He makes his way up and plays with Mike's beard. Even though it's soft and downy, it's handsome.

Luke starts to go in for a kiss. Mike senses it and opens his eyes. Mike whispers, "I really like the jerking, but that's all I'm interested in." He smiles at Luke. Luke gets the message and diverts his mouth to Mike's nipple. Mike growls and Luke nibbles on it; Mike puts his hand on Luke's head and tousles his hair. "Yeah, that's good," Mike growls at Luke.

Tom gets up, rubbing his knees from the hard tile. "Would you like to finish somewhere more comfortable? No funny stuff, we promise."

Mike says, "Sure."

They dry off and head back to their room. The boys get the mattress back on the floor. Mike lays down, and Luke crawls between his legs. Luke is leaking up a storm enjoying sucking Mike's thick cock, even though he can only get a little more than half in his mouth. Luke then thinks about Rob. He's even thicker. He hopes he gets a chance to test his skills on Rob one day. While lost in thought, he doesn't notice Tom has gotten the lube out. Luke feels a finger inserted into his hole. Luke moans as it slips in. He and Tom have experimented a bit more with each other and some toys. Luke has really learned to relax and enjoy.

Tom leans over Luke and whispers, "Are you ready to finally get fucked properly?" Luke nods and moans an affirmative, never removing Mike's fat cock from his mouth. Tom aims his cock, and gently slides all the way in. Luke makes a grunt from the momentary sensation of being stretched open.

Mike opens his eyes. "Whoa...that's kind of hot." Mike grabs a pillow to prop his head up so he can watch Luke get spit roasted. With every slow thrust Tom makes, Luke becomes more insatiable on Mike's cock. Luke manages to get another inch or so of Mike's cock in his mouth. Tom picks up speed as he senses Luke loosening up. Mike holds Luke's head and makes little thrusts. Luke uses one hand on Mike's balls and another on a nipple. Mike growls with every twist. Tom is turned on by how much of Mike's cock Luke has gotten in his mouth, and watching Mike slowly, gently thrust. The site is sending him over the edge. Tom grabs Luke's hips and thrusts harder. Luke Moans with every thrust. Mike moves faster, careful not to choke him while working on the cum boiling up from his big balls. "I'm gonna cum, buddy."

Luke nods and moans in acceptance. Tom yells, "Fuck, yeah. Take that load, Luke. I'm gonna bury mine in your ass, too."

As if in sync. Tom and Mike both throw their heads back and moan loudly as they fill Luke from both ends. Luke's cock erupts without being touched. Mike's cum is so much that Luke can't swallow it all. It runs down his chin from around Mike's shaft. He can feel Tom's cum running down his balls as it leaks out while Tom continues to pound. Luke's own cock is still pulsing from his orgasm, even though he ran out of jizz after the sixth spurt. They begin to slow their collective thrusts as their orgasms subside.

As they both pull out, Luke collapses on his side. He's a cum-covered mess and never felt so satisfied. Mike is the first to speak. "Damn. That was incredible. I didn't think I'd ever be able to get a blow job, let alone one that amazing. I like pussy when I can get it, but damn, you gay boys know how to suck a dick."

The boys laugh. Luke says, "Anytime you need a hand."

Tom adds, "Or mouth." They all laugh.

After Mike leaves, the boys go to rinse the sex off in the shower. Luke wipes off with a towel first, so he's not too suspicious if they run into someone in the hall. Luke says, "I wonder what it'd be like to get fucked by one that big."

Tom laughs, "Slow down, power bottom in the making." They both laugh. "Did you enjoy it tonight? Getting fucked?"

Luke looks incredulous, "Do you have to ask? I came without touching my dick."

Tom says, "I just thought that was from choking on Mike's fat cock."

Luke laughs. "That may have helped a little." They laugh again.

Tom says more seriously, "Big dicks require working up to it. You should also make sure it's a top that understands the pain and damage they could cause. Some guys are rough and don't care. Be careful when the opportunity finally comes around for a big one." Luke nods, understanding.

❧ II ❧

CHAMPIONSHIP

Luke has really enjoyed his first semester at college. He and Tom are best friends with benefits. Tom has taught him a lot, and Luke feels comfortable in his own skin for the first time in his life. Tom's helping him develop his gaydar. They hook up with two other students they'd met. Tom shows him the ropes on how and where to cruise. Second-floor library bathroom, where they met the first student (the second is in one of Tom's classes). The cross-country trails for meeting up and what signals to look for. The gym, of course, which is more difficult for Luke since he works there. They know about the dirty bookstore two towns over but have never explored it. Tom tells Luke he'd read online that the rest area off the interstate could be as well, but neither of them has braved it.

Most of Luke's limited experiences happen at the river. There's a sandbar in a small river not too far away where people like to hang out on weekends. Tom shows Luke the trails that lead upriver to a bank in a bend where people sunbathe nude and the cruising that happens further in the woods on the trails. This mostly leads to some jerk sessions, some of those while watching other men suck and fuck. A few BJs from a variety of ages, some much older. As winter approaches and the weather gets cooler, studies take over, and Luke's schedule becomes more class, study, practice, work, match.

⁂

As the semester nears its end, the season's final match is here. The tournament is held at a large athletic center. The facilities are nice, with multiple locker rooms to accommodate such events. Most of his teammates have early matches. Luke is in line to rank 1st in the state in class, so his first match isn't in the first few rounds. He's feeling the pressure a bit before the match, knowing that winning might help him with scholarships for a four-year college.

Luke has been following Coach's suggestion of 'exercising' ("My right arm," Luke thinks to himself) right before each match. It's really helped him keep his unwanted public erections under control this season. He starts his routine in a bathroom stall, like usual. He always begins by rubbing his nipple through the material of his singlet until his dick is hard. The strain of the singlet against his cock feels wonderful. Eventually, he pulls his singlet to the side to access his cock and balls. Getting hard, like always, is easy enough. Today, though, he is too distracted by the realities of the finals and can't seem to accomplish his goal of emptying his balls to get out to the mats. He hears Coach calling his name from the locker room. He realizes how long he's probably been in the stall. He can hear Coach right outside the stall, realizing that his shoes gave away his location.

"What's the problem, son?" Luke's cock throbs at Coach calling him son. He's always thought of Coach as a father figure. That's something new to process.

Luke says softly through the crank in the door. "I can't seem to finish, uh, 'exercising.' And been trying for a while. And it's definitely not going down," he finishes frantically.

"I feel sorry for you, kid. I truly sympathize. But what do you want me to do about it? You've got 15 minutes or so before the next round starts."

After a pause, Luke leans closer to the door. "Can you...can you help me?"

Coach chuckles, "I love you, kid, but I'm not risking my job for you."

In a higher-than-normal voice, Luke says, "What should I do?"

Coach looks around. The locker room is mostly empty, just the occasional person coming back for something they forgot. It's early in the tournament, so most people are out watching or participating on the floor. He turns back towards the door. "Make your way to the last stall. I'll see if I can get some help."

Luke wipes the precum from his tip before pulling his singlet back over his erection, not that it's hiding much, but he knows he can't walk out of the stall with his boner pointing straight out at anyone who might walk by. He walks down to the last stall, the farthest away from the door. He's not sure why Coach has sent him down to this stall, but he realizes he probably should have done that to begin with, just in case someone noticed what he was doing.

He begins to stroke again, removing his cock from his singlet so he doesn't get a wet spot. His eyes close, concentrating on the sensations his strokes give his cock. He's so close to cumming, but he just can't make it happen. He's jarred to his senses when he hears the stall door next to him shut and lock. He wonders who it is. The thought turns him on. He thinks about how Coach knew it was him in the stall by his feet. He tilts his head and sees black shower shoes. It could be anyone; the majority of his team has those same ones. It's likely that most people at the tournament do, too.

"Even Coach has those kind," Luke begins to wonder but is interrupted by the feet as they turn and face towards him. Luke can hear some light scraping on the cubicle wall.

Luke doesn't know what to make of the situation. Just as he starts to wonder if he should worry, the toilet paper holder slides out of the way, revealing a hole between the stalls. "Oh," Luke thinks, "this must be a glory hole. Tom told me about these, but I didn't think I'd ever see one. Especially in a place as fancy as this facility." Luke then realizes the TP holders are rigged together on both sides to hide it so it doesn't get repaired. Luke wakes from his thoughts to discover that two fingers are tapping the bottom of the hole. Luke's not sure what that means. He hears the other person clear his throat and tap again slower. Luke realizes he's supposed to put his cock through. He puts it all the way through, his chest and belly flat to the wall, his head turned to the side. A warm mouth engulfs his cock. He stifles a moan. An expert tongue goes to work.

The oral skills of the cocksucker are exceptional, but Luke realizes the situation is making it even more erotic. Luke understands the stories he's learned over the last few months of the "days of old" cruising. Luke begins to thrust, his hands flat on the wall, wishing they could hold the back of the head sucking him. Luke can feel his balls finally starting to draw up, preparing to empty into a willing mouth. The guy on the other side of the wall notices, too, because he grabs Luke's balls and pulls down against their natural ascension. The sensation is just what Luke needs to push him over the edge. Luke bites his hand to muffle the scream of ecstasy as his load is finally purged. As the pulses subside, he feels a hand wrap around the base of his shaft to squeeze every last drop into the mouth still wrapped about his cock. Luke pulls his cock out of the hole. It's mostly limp already from the intense orgasm. He gets his cock and balls tucked in his singlet and leans towards the opening, whispering, "Thank you." He hears an affirmative "um hm" in response as he opens the door and runs towards the mats, hearing his name being called over the speakers for the next round.

❈

LUKE STEPS DOWN FROM THE PODIUM, A 1ST PLACE state champion medal around his neck. Tom places 2nd in his class. Another guy from their team got 3rd in his. The whole team is hugging and patting each other on the back. They all make their way to the locker room to shower and change, ready for celebrations before the bus ride home. Luke is lagging behind, exhausted from the mental stresses of the day. The match and what happened before. A familiar, gentle hand lands on his shoulder, "I'm proud of you, son. You did great out there."

He looks up over his shoulder at Coach and smiles. Luke stands, "Thanks for everything, Coach."

"It was nothing. You put in all the work." Luke smiles, "That, too. But I meant earlier."

Coach blinks at him, "I didn't do anything." Coach pauses, realizing it's not registering. "I just told you to be at the right place and hoped for the best."

Luke's jaw drops, stunned that it had been a random stranger.

Coach winks, "It does help to know where the action happens." He shrugs as if to feign modesty. He smacks Luke lightly on the bum, sending him off to the showers. As Luke walks away, he thinks, "Note to self: find more glory holes."

IV
ENJAMBMENT

by Peter Schutes

PUBLISHER'S NOTE

This work of erotic fiction is one of the last stories written by Peter before he died in 1981 at 85 years old. It is set in his adopted city, Los Angeles, in the present, which was 1980. Its language and expressions are modern. The story deals with modern themes, like sexual hypnosis, exercise and fitness, and the cult of body worship that became synonymous with the 1980s in the wake of Olivia Newton John's "Physical." It is a testament to his skill as a writer that he captured this moment in time so precisely.

ENJAMBMENT

I have always been into learning new things. I guess I'm just naturally curious. One day while searching in the UCLA Library, I stumble upon a book about hypnosis that captures my curiosity. I have long been interested in mind control and other forms of domination. This book is particularly interesting because it has a significant section on seduction through "covert hypnosis."

Covert hypnosis is related to a poetic term I learned in a night school class on modern poetry: enjambment. In poetry, enjambment is incomplete syntax at the end of a line; the meaning is carried over from one poetic line to the next. The classic example is from T S Eliot's The Waste Land:

> April is the cruelest month, breeding
> Lilacs out of the dead land...

YOU WILL NOTICE THAT YOU CANNOT TELL WHERE the verse is going until you get to the second line. Covert hypnosis borrows from this principle by embedding a hypnotic command within two ordinary sentences. A classic example is

> I can see that you are hot.
> For me, this heat is pretty tolerable.

Embedded in there is the statement/command, "You are hot for me." According to this covert hypnosis expert, if you can do this naturally, the command will slip directly into your subject's unconscious without them realizing it. Suddenly, they will wonder why they feel hot for you!

This sounds too good to be true, so I decide to test it out at the country club on a very fit straight lad who seems to be a little curious about me and my massive bulge. I should point out that I have enormous balls and a very thick cock, both of which are hard to hide when I'm working my thighs on the leg press or doing jumping jacks. I have seen him glancing surreptitiously at my package, so he must want to know a little more. I've spoken with him before, but I could never pique his interest other than a few sneaky peeks below my belt. He did tell me his name was Darryl, and he has a girlfriend that lives with him.

I've told Darryl I live alone on Wilshire, just a few blocks from the country club, so he knows a little about me. He probably works early hours because I usually run into him in the weight room on a weekday just before rush hour.

I want to see if I can convince him to fuck me using nothing more than the power of covert hypnosis. I know my dick is way too thick for all but the most experienced bottom men, so it is more realistic to focus on landing him as a Greek active. Besides, he has massive arms and a powerful chest, with glutes and back muscles designed for thrusting in and out of any hole.

Until now, I have only managed to have brief, casual conversations with Darryl.

To prepare, I think up as many covert hypnotic commands as possible and write them down. I studied them and memorized them all week. I get off early on Fridays, so that was the day I picked to test the technique on Darryl. As the week progressed, I got hotter and hotter thinking about how I was going to seduce this muscle man!

Friday afternoon, as soon as I get home, I put on my light grey gym shorts with neither jockstrap nor briefs. The shorts are made of thin, shiny nylon, assuring a visible genital jiggle on the treadmill. Here's where my story begins.

As I walk into the gym, I notice Darryl jogging on an older model of manual treadmill. Perfect! There is only one other machine like it, and they are side by side. I head over to the empty machine. Unlike the latest electric models, it uses only gravity, so it takes effort to get started. After a minute, I lightly jog, forcing my thick meat to swing side to side. It looks like two squirrels fighting beneath the fabric of my shorts.

Darryl immediately glances down and takes a long, curious look. I smile to myself, knowing that I have a whole toolbox to turn that natural curiosity into unbridled lust.

The first rule of covert hypnosis is to confuse the subject momentarily before beginning. This works best if you use a run-on sentence. I start my seduction:

"Darryl! What's up?"

"Hey, Pete."

"If there were ever any air conditioning in this place, it would have been turned up to eleven, and we still would be shivering like a boar in a boxcar full of witches' teats."

Darryl frowns and gets a glazed look in his eyes. Then he says, "Yeah, it's hot in here."

Time for my first covert suggestion. I start with that old saw, "I can see that you are hot. For me, this heat is pretty tolerable."

"I know; I'm really sweating, huh?" Darryl wipes his forehead.

I say, "Yes, you are! Very curious,"

After that sentence, I glance at his crotch, which looks like a pretty fulsome piece of meat. He glances at mine almost automatically. He is getting more curious, just like my last sentence implanted in his mind.

My copy of the Times is open to the stocks. I tap the page. "Time to get your buy order in for GE stock." [Notice how "You're bi" is buried in there.]

Darryl looks at the paper, "I don't follow the markets, but maybe I should." He laughs at himself.

"Oh yes, Darryl, you really should. Fuck! Me, I had a hard year of it." [Now it's your turn to find the embedded suggestions!]

"Oh really, what happened?"

Not every sentence has to be a seduction - that can get pretty ridiculous. "I bought this stock at a huge discount to value, thinking it would go up, but it just flatlined and then plummeted."

"I don't even know what that means, but maybe I should find out."

"It's quite simple to show you how to do it. With me, you'll learn."

"I really want to learn."

"If you see something you want to, do it! To me, that's a good philosophy."

Darryl is looking at my bouncing junk again. Did I see him lick his lips? Is this actually working? I continue.

"I'll bet you are that type. You see an open door, and you want to enter. Me, I like to try anything and everything I can. I can give you a quickie lesson on the market after this if you like."

Darryl nods, his eyes wandering toward my ass. Is this working? He seems a bit dazed.

Maybe it's all the endorphins.

I try another one on him: "You can come to my place and learn this stuff if you want. What you see isn't gonna make much sense when you're on a treadmill."

"Yeah, a bunch of noise," Darryl agrees but doesn't know what he's agreeing to.

"And you never know what you're getting. Hard to predict, really."

"Oh, you mean the market reports? Yeah, liars."

When I look at Darryl's crotch this time, he really is getting hard. Damn, this stuff is brilliant!

"Still, money is something you always want to watch. It's getting harder and harder to avoid."

"Like all that Inflation bullshit." Darryl is trying to follow me, but the sentences are awkward in places. I take this opportunity to put both my hands at the top of my glutes while I look at Darryl's.

"Damn, man, you must work out pretty hard."

Darryl smiles at the compliment. "Yeah. I'm here like every day. I hardly ever see you."

"I come here a little later. What can I say? My ass is here now. For you, it's probably easier because of your work schedule."

Darryl looks at my ass again. "Yep, your ass is here." Now I'm detecting a little desire on the edge of his words.

Careful not to fall off the elliptical, I lift my shirt. "Let me see your abs."

Darryl looks at my furry belly while he lifts his shirt to reveal a total 8-pack.

"I wish I had your 8-pack abs. Next to mine, yours are so hard. For me, that is a huge accomplishment."

To attempt to break the spell, he mentions Lisa, his

girlfriend. "I've been with Lisa for two years this week. Oh shit! I almost forgot our anniversary."

"You know, I'm really good at giving gifts. I can help you find something. That would be nice, right?"

Darryl is still beating himself up. "I'm so stupid!"

"An anniversary is something that sometimes you just forget all about. Lisa will understand."

My seeds have been planted, so I step off the old treadmill. Darryl is still going.

He looks me up and down, "Dude, are you serious about that offer to help me pick out something?"

Time to start closing the deal, "Yeah, totally. We can do it right after this, except are you hungry?"

"Nah. Well, maybe a little."

"You need to eat, man, fuck! Me, I'm hungry, too. We can get something at my place."

"Oh yeah, you're just up the block, right?" His treadmill stops as he dismounts.

"Right up the block. You can come over. Me, I walk. What about you?"

"I drive."

Well, I certainly have gotten pretty far with Darryl. These secret hypnotic suggestions have conspired to force him to let his guard down. We wipe down our machines and our sweaty foreheads.

"I'm on the 12th floor of the Westwood on Wilshire. Do you know it? Will feel good to eat, right?"

"Oh, I parked near there today. Let's walk. Now that you mention it, I'm pretty hungry." As he says this, Darryl is looking right at my ass. Then he comes out of left field.

"Dude, I gotta ask, what is the deal with your bulge?"

"You mean my cock and balls?"

"Yeah, your bulge."

"I was kind of hoping you would ask about my ass."

He laughs at my comment. "I'm just curious." (Damn right you are)

"I tell you what, we can both shower when we get back to my place. I'll bet you would like that."

Darryl grins sheepishly.

We walk the four blocks or so to my apartment. No sooner are we inside my door than he lifts off his shirt and throws it to the ground, revealing a perfectly sculpted chest with big burly arms. He has a light dusting of fur that belies the testosterone naturally coursing through his system. I just stare in awe and disbelief.

He steps forward, pulling off my shirt and rubbing my furry belly with his big meaty paws. All my embedded suggestions are coming to the surface now. "Dude, I don't know why I feel like this, but I just want to eat your ass so bad right now!"

I drop my shorts, revealing my bubble butt and my clunky junk. Darryl is staring in astonishment. My cock is too thick and not quite long enough to fuck most people, so I usually choose to bottom instead. But Darryl is a little size queen, and he just looks and looks before he says, "Damn, dude, not only do you have a super-fat shorty, you got fucking huge balls."

"Go on and touch them if you want." I'm getting hard, and I can see Darryl's sausage poking forward in his shorts. "But first, you gotta take off your shorts, too."

Darryl obliges, revealing a perfect waist with those lines etched at the base of the abdominals leading to his cock. I underestimated his cock, which is both a grower and a shower. He was maybe 4 inches semi-hard; I'd thought he would be average, but I was wrong. Now it's growing and growing, past six inches, then past seven, while the girth grows from nice and easy to holy shit size.

Now it's my turn, "Dude, your cock is fucking huge!"

Darryl grins in agreement. "You think you can take it?"

I swallow hard before answering, "I know I can."

Now Darryl is in charge, and I'm all too happy to let him take over. This may not be his first time at the rodeo.

He lifts me and lays me face up on the kitchen counter. He puts one leg on each shoulder, working his tongue across my balls and into my hole. I start wriggling with pleasure, hardly able to contain the excitement. He spends a good three minutes on my ass, loosening it and lubing it up with his spit. I cast a surreptitious glance below his waist to see if he is still into it. He's throbbing, hard as a rock.

The kitchen counter is above waist level, so there will have to be a change of venue if this is going all the way. I consider saying something to Darryl, but he's one step ahead. With his big jock arms, he picks me up at the waist and carries all 200 pounds of me over to the kitchen table, laying me down among the placemats and unread mail. His cock is lying across my thigh now, still hard but succumbing to the pressures of a full corpus cavernosum and gravity.

"You gotta suck it before I will fuck it."

"Bring it here." He walks around the table to my open and willing mouth. He points my chin up in the air and goes straight in upside down. I can only see his chiseled thighs and his balls. They are heavy with cum and pretty big but dwarfed by his massive cock. They are nowhere near as big as mine, but that's a blessing. As he fucks my mouth, those balls slap against my nose and eyes.

Darryl is a considerate lover. He asks before attempting to deep throat. I have listened to hours of hypnosis tapes to reduce my gag reflex and have become an expert cocksucker, but this will be the triathlon of deep-throating. I open my mouth as wide as it will go so Darryl's cock only grazes my lips and tongue. To stimulate his cock, he will have to push past my tonsils and into my esophagus. And he does. I gag a little, but nothing like I used to before I did that Deep Throat hypnosis. God bless Linda Lovelace for teaching us fags how it works.

Darryl is hugely impressed with my cocksucking skills. "Pete, you are fucking unreal. I don't know anyone who can do that without puking. Not even Lisa."

The mention of his girlfriend worries me a little, but Darryl keeps thrusting in and out. "You want me to shoot a load down your throat?"

I shake my head no. I can't answer aloud, not with my throat rhythmically stuffed with a pound and a half of cock.

"Why not? Oh, you want it in the ass, huh?"

I nod and manage to blurt out an "uh-huh" between thrusts.

Darryl is starting to breathe heavily. "Don't worry, dude. I got at least two loads in here. I'm gonna cum in your mouth."

He pulls his cock out of my throat. "Shoot in my mouth. I want to taste it." I begin giving the amateur head that most girlfriends give, sucking and licking, using my lips instead of my tonsils to stimulate the sides of his cock.

"Dude, oh shit, oh shit!" Darryl suddenly stops thrusting and tenses his muscles before unleashing a flood of cum. I have had Tiger Bars with less nutrition than this soup of DNA and body fluids. I swallow as fast as I can, but it comes too quickly, spilling out the sides of my mouth. I catch the drips with my cupped hand as Darryl pulls his still-hard cock out of my mouth. I lift my hand towards my mouth to finish off the meal, but Darryl grabs my wrist and slurps his own cum out of my hand.

Without missing a beat, Darryl walks around the table and starts licking my asshole again. It's still pretty lubed up with his slippery spit. He licks my ass cheeks, lapping up the sweat from our little workout.

"Dude, I'm serious. No one can take my cock down their throat. I always try, and they can't. You're gonna see a lot more of me."

"Practice and training," I croak hoarsely.

"Lisa won't let me give it to her in the butt. Are you gonna let me?"

"Yeah, I'm gonna take that whole fucking thing, man." I spread my ass cheeks to encourage him.

He shakes his head like he's trying to startle a fly out of his hair. "Damn, that is one fucking beautiful ass. You know that?"

"I haven't seen it straight on. But I'll take your word for it."

"Take this," Darryl says as he pushes the head of his cock against my sphincter.

Now, I've been gang-banged, fucked silly, and I think I'm pretty experienced with anal sex. Darryl has one of those cruel cocks that gets thicker and thicker from the head to the base. The further he thrusts in, the wider your sphincter has to spread. This can be a painful experience unless you can relax into it. I think to myself, 'Deep Hypno Sleep,' and I find myself entering trance, where relaxation is easy.

He pushes his cock head past my sphincter and starts to fill my rectum. He knows his cruel cock pretty well because he's careful to take it nice and slow, allowing my asshole to adjust and accommodate the ever-increasing girth. I moan with anticipation.

"Am I hurting you, dude?" He looks very concerned. I can see that he hasn't been with many anal enthusiasts. I'll bet he's heard 'take it out!' and 'nope, never mind' a lot in his life.

"You're fucking huge. I hope you're hurting me. That's part of the experience!"

"Wait, you don't want me to pull out?" Poor guy, he must face a lot of this rejection.

"I'm saying I want you to force your cock all the way up inside me and then start fucking me silly."

That's all he needs. He goes all the way in with one violent thrust, stretching my rectum and sphincter to the point of deep pain. I cry out in agony, but it quickly dissolves into moans of pleasure.

With each forward thrust, my asshole gets stretched to its limit, and with each outstroke, I feel relief. He's fucking me slowly and deliberately, like an oil derrick. He's afraid he might break me. I understand his hesitation. No one has ever successfully let me fuck them, and Darryl has no doubt faced some of this rejection as well.

"Fuck me harder." Darryl picks up the pace a notch, but it's still pretty slow. I want him to know what it's like to fuck with wild abandon.

"Harder!" Now he's moving fast. I slap his ass, and he picks up the pace some more. I gasp, cry out, and moan, but I make sure there's a smile on my face the whole time. I don't want him to stop because he thinks I'm not able to take him.

As Darryl thrusts his hips, I feel his balls slapping against mine. Each time he pushes forward, they swing into my backside and tickle my bottom. His thighs slap against my ass cheeks, making it sound like someone is spanking me. Still in a light trance, I know this has got to be one of the most pleasurable fucks in my life. Darryl is young, but he's an expert ass-fucker.

Looking at him from this angle, he's a magnificent beast of a man. Sweat trickles down the canyon between his pectoral muscles, each crowned with perfect, large nipples. I reach up to play with those nipples. Darryl moans softly and gives off a wave of sexual energy that engulfs us both.

I start to feel a tingling along the walls of my butthole. That hypnosis tape that trained me to have anal orgasms is kicking in. I look at Darryl, sweat dripping from his brow, and run my hands along his chest, stroking his nipples again. He wiggles when I touch them. As I start to move towards his perfect abs, he says, "Pinch them. My nipples."

I obey, running little circles around them and giving them a surprise tug every few seconds. There is a powerful force in this blissful union. Darryl's tingling nipples send energy down my fingers and into my anus, where the orgasm is building. The battery that powers this source comes from Darryl's thrusting hips and his huge cock filling my hole.

We both feel it, and it completes the circuit when we look each other in the eye. I start to explode, first in my ass, then my dick. Without touching it, my cock shoots ropy strands of cum onto Darryl's chest and mine.

"Fu-u-u-u-ck yeah!" Darryl cries out. The energy exchange has sent him over the edge, and he explodes inside my ass, where the walls are still throbbing with anal orgasm. I reach up my head and lap up some of the cum I sprayed on Darryl's chest. He shakes with pleasure at the new sensation of a tongue on his skin. He returns the favor, licking the semen from my belly and chest. He's still inside me, and I feel him tense his cock to squeeze out the last droplets.

He pulls his cock out of my ass, and it lands on the kitchen table like a catfish, making a heavy "thunk" sound. Semi-hard, it must weigh two pounds.

We both breathe heavily, like two fighters who reached the end of a match. Neither of us says anything for fear of ruining the moment.

I get down from the table and take his cock into my mouth, cleaning it and making it hard again.

"Now it's your turn," he says.

I shake my head wearily and point to my cock. "It doesn't fit in your mouth, and it sure as hell won't fit in your ass."

"I need a good fuck, dude. I need it bad - bad enough to take that monster." He leans back on the table and raises his legs, presenting his tight anus like a friendly gibbon.

To my surprise, my cock is already hard again. Darryl is spitting into his hand and rubbing spit onto his fuckhole. I smile and shake my head. "Spit ain't gonna cut it, man."

I open the cupboard above the fridge and take down a tub of Crisco. Darryl is too straight to know what it means.

"Are you going to fry some chicken? Come on, fuck me!"

I can sometimes fuck a guy if he gets fisted first, so that is the angle I'm going for. I don't think he'll go that far, but it's worth a try. "I can make fried chicken. If you want, there's a whole fryer in the fridge. This is not for chicken. Do you want to guess what Crisco can do for you?"

"Uh, make pie crust?"

"This is gonna loosen up your hole if you let me."

"Dude, I love anything up my ass. Fuckin' do whatever you want." He flashes me a pearly white grin that could melt a tub of shortening.

I take a generous tablespoon of Crisco and put it right on his hole. It's room temperature, but it still feels cold to Darryl, and he jumps. I put two fingers together and start to push into his ass. He must play with toys at home because he doesn't jump like every other straight guy I've touched there.

"Oh damn, that's some slippery shit."

I nod and continue to work my two fingers into his hole, gently parting them to stretch his sphincter. He's clearly done this before. Maybe Lisa straps it on.

"Pete, that feels fucking amazing. Don't stop."

"Oh, I won't." I grin and slip a third finger in his hole. He winces for a second like I knew he would. This is usually where people draw the line.

"Dude, are you going to put your whole hand in there?" Darryl looks curious, not frightened.

"Only if you let me."

"Hell yeah! Try anything once!" He lies back like a patient at a doctor's and lets me work his hole. I add my pinky to the mix. He doesn't notice or doesn't care.

I have a significant barrier to overcome - the thumb. I decide to use a little hypnotic induction on him to make it possible.

"Feels good, doesn't it?"

"Yeah, kinda tight, but it feels good." I put a clean finger to his lips to shush him.

"Let me talk you through this. Just lie back and don't say anything. It will make this feel really good."

"Okay." He looks up at the ceiling.

"You're looking at a point on the ceiling. Keep looking at it, and don't blink unless I tell you to." Darryl obediently gazes at his spot on the ceiling.

"As you gaze at that spot, you notice that the muscles around your eyes that usually hold so much tension are just starting to relax. You may even notice that your eyelids feel heavy, and you want to blink. Go ahead and blink." Darryl blinks. "Now that you blinked, those muscles are feeling even more loose and lazy. That relaxation in your eyes is spreading down your chest, along your arms, and around your waist. Every muscle relaxing and feeling loose and lazy. Your eye muscles might even want to rest and allow your eyelids to shut." As expected, Darryl is a really easy subject, and his eyes close. He moans softly with pleasure as I work my four fingers in and out of his hole.

I continue to induce trance, taking him deeper, snapping my fingers. I command him to open his eyes but remain in trance, which he does. I snap my fingers, and he immediately falls back into a deep sleep. But I want him to enjoy the experience, so I set him in a state of trance where he will feel his muscles relaxing in his asshole, but he will remember every experience. Pain will be 1/10th of what it usually is, and pleasure will be multiplied ten times. And then that little bit of discomfort is now only 1/100 of what it was. And pleasure is multiplied 100 times. He's there. I tell him that when I snap my fingers, my thumb goes into his ass to join those four fingers, and he wants them to be together. He nods in agreement.

Snap! My thumb slides in like a pig in a chute. Darryl moans with pleasure. I have implanted a suggestion that when he is ready for me to put my knuckles in there, he should just let me know.

"Dude, put those knuckles in." I oblige, and voilà, I'm wrist-deep in Darryl. He moans and moans, but it isn't pain. He's in ecstasy. He starts humping my arm, and his flaccid penis begins to grow again and stand at attention. He's ready.

"Do you want me to put this fucking short fat beer can of a cock into you?"

"Yes, sir." I haven't implanted any submissive suggestions, but he seems to prefer that when he's under.

"I want you to see it go in. Lift your head so you can see my cock."

Darryl's mouth waters, and he says, "Dude, that's a fucking huge cock."

"It is. It's too huge for you. I'm not going to put it in you."

Darryl's face falls like a three-year-old being denied a pixie stick. "You're not?"

"No, I can't put it in unless you convince me you are able to handle it."

"I have your arm up my ass; I think I can take your dick." Good point. Darryl should be in Sales.

"All right then, I'm going to put it in. But you can ask me to take it out at any time.

"Yes, sir. Fuck me, sir." Darryl's submissive act is a big turn-on. My cock is rock hard. It is 4.5 inches long with the girth of a beer can. It is a freaky cock, but it's mine.

I remove my hand slowly from Darryl's ass, watching the sphincter gape like the entrance to a cavern. I position Darryl's ass close to my hips and put the fat head of my cock against the opening. I know he took my fist, but this will still hurt. It's shaped differently, and he doesn't know the agony it can inflict.

"What are you waiting for, sir? Put it in me."

Any misgivings fall to the wayside, and I pop the head of my cock through his opening. His eyes widen with pain. He grunts and winces.

"Take it out?" I ask.

"No, man, fuck me like we said."

I grab his thighs and pull his ass onto my dick. It's completely cylindrical, so there is no moment of relief when you get past a particular spot - it's just non-stop pain. Darryl's eyes are watering, and I start to think he's going to give up when something amazing happens.

I can feel Darryl squeeze my cock with his ass muscles. I look down at him, and he is grinning. "See, I told you I could take it. Now fuck the shit out of me."

I oblige, thrusting in and out with reckless abandon. I keep checking Darryl's face to see if he is suffering, but he is in nirvana.

"Dude, your cock feels so good up there. I fucking love it." Darryl is a jock, and I guess jocks enjoy a certain amount of pain. They get hurt so often when they play rough sports. Darryl should be awarded a medal.

It isn't the length that makes a cock painful; it's the width. Darryl's cock has both, but mine is the same volume as his, with all the length added to the width instead. It's a beast of a cock, and I can't believe I am fucking the hottest guy at the gym, and he isn't crying out for mercy.

I don't want this to end. Darryl looks like he could go all night. His cock is semi-hard. I think he deserves to be hard during this, so I reach down and play with his nipples. His cock stands to attention, and his eyes widen.

"Dude, that makes me blow my load. Are you ready for that?"

In response, I lower my head and take the head of his cock into my mouth. I keep playing with his nipples, and he squeezes hard on my cock with his ass muscles. We made a new circuit this time, with my mouth, his nipples, and my cock up his ass. Energy starts to flow. I speed up my thrusts, tasting the precum leaking from Darryl's cock. His moans become wails. I wonder what the neighbors will think, briefly, and then put the thought out of my mind to focus on Darryl's nipples, face, cock, and ass.

Warm Crisco is gently oozing from the edges of Darryl's ass - melted by all the friction. I can feel it running down my leg like butter dripping off toast. His cock has reached its python-like dimensions, and I can take the first three inches into my mouth, so I do. I diddle his nipples and watch his face contort like a bodybuilder lifting 250 pounds. Then his face softens.

"Pete, I'm gonna fucking come. I'm gonna come." To reassure him, I suck his cock harder, tasting the sweet precum oozing faster and faster. The precum sends me near the edge, and I buck and thrust.

Darryl grabs my ass and pulls me close to him, forcing my cock inside him balls deep. He moans and gasps, then makes the 'gonna come' face. I feel a gush of cum fill my mouth. This time, I manage to slurp it all down. His cock softens, and I let it hit his chest with a resounding "thump." He is coming out of his trance, and I'm still inside him, thrusting. But Darryl pulls me closer and says, "I want your cum, man. I want to say I took your cock and earned your cum."

That's it; it's the right words to put me right over. To think of my cum as a trophy for this muscle man turns me on. To realize that this little man just let me fist him and fuck him silly sends waves of pleasure coursing through my muscles and down to my beer-can cock. The floodgates open. I am so used to coming with my hand as a bottom that I've forgotten what this feels like. I think I could water all my houseplants with the cum spurting out of my cock right now, deep inside Darryl's ass. I moan and sigh, squeezing out the last drops.

We stay like this for a good minute, breathing, Darryl smiling up at me, his liquid trophy inside him. Finally, I back away, and my cock falls right out of his slick, Crisco-ed asshole. Darryl leaps up and cleans my dick with his mouth, looking for and finding the remnants of my sperm. His ass is so loose; it's dripping and forming a puddle of cum on the floor.

Like a dog on all fours, Darryl backs up and laps up the puddle, holding a cupped hand to catch the cum and melted Crisco still spilling from him. He lifts the brew towards his lips, but I grab his wrist; we share the cum and shortening stew.

While I fix us some sandwiches, we chitchat just like we do in the weight room at the club: small talk, the sports page.

"You still want to learn about the markets? I forgot the paper at the club, but I have some old ones lying around."

"I'm a meathead. I don't give a shit about the stock market. I just wanted to fuck your pretty ass."

Then I remember something Darryl said in the heat of passion and ask him, "You said that you wanted to be able to say that you took my cock and earned my cum. I'm just wondering...who would you say that to?"

"Oh, to the other guys at the gym. We've all seen the way your cock shakes your shorts, and we had a running bet about who could seduce you and take you full term to sperm without quitting. I was the first one. I won!"

"The first?"

"Dude, I took that fucking beer can like a professional. There is no way I'm letting the other guys walk away from this challenge. Which one you wanna fuck next? I'll set it up."

ABOUT THE AUTHORS

Peter Schutes (1896-1981) began writing when he found a typewriter at a Montana bunkhouse in the early 1950s. He had a "big problem." He wrote smut focused mainly on matters of size. Peter's prolific volumes of steamy men's tales were some of the finest gay pulp fiction to grace the shelves of dirty bookstores. As a bonus note: Peter is entirely and utterly fictitious. His legendary schlong lives in the waters of Loch Ness.

Peter Schutes is the nom de plume of a prolific and acclaimed novelist. As Peter Schutes, he is the author of Adult Erotic Fiction such as <u>The Slaves of Rome</u>, <u>Dark as a Dungeon</u>, <u>The Gospel of Priapus</u>, and <u>Panama Heat</u>. He writes in the style of vintage pulp authors from the 1960s and 1970s. He lives in Los Angeles.

Chuck Idgaf is a relatively new queer author. Deep into middle age, Chuck decided to broaden his hobbies, writing very erotic short stories. Initially, he just shared them with friends. The collaboration with Jim Dandy is the first time his work will be widely available. Chuck has a fondness for bears and daddies, so those tend to be common themes. He also likes stories about coming out, first times, and exploring new experiences. If you can't figure it out from the dialogue in his stories, Chuck grew up in the Deep South. He now lives in the Coachella Valley, California, with his husband.

OTHER BOOKS FROM PETER SCHUTES PUBLISHING

E-books and Paperbacks

The Able Seaman

The Anaconda Copper

The Autobiography of Peter Schutes

Backwoods Delivery

Big Hole River

Bobbing Buoys and Salty Seamen

Bunkhouse Buddies

The Butt Baby

Cloistered

Confessions of a Rodeo Clown

Dark as a Dungeon

Demonic Deception *aka* Deceived, Cursed & Blessed

Desert Island Daddies

Dirty Dorms and Fresh Men

The Expectant Member

Firehouse Lovers

The Fish

Five Erotic Tales

The Gospel of Priapus

Hercules and Lippos

Hobo Honey

Hot Blue Collars

Hotshot

Logger's Delight

Muscle Bottom

Panama Heat

Satanic Seductions

Satan's Sissy Boy

The Slaves of Rome

The Thigh Baby

Under the Boardwalk

World's Biggest

***** Coming Soon *****

Like the Greeks Do

Hoboes, Hustlers, and Jailbirds

Small Cockpits and Big Hangars

Tales of Two Daddies

More Tales of Two Daddies